Deselections

Deselections

[From The Hagiography of a Disc Jockey]

To David
Enjoy,
My Apologies

K Hank Jost

SPARK SPUTTER & DIE

Whisk(e)y Tit
NYC & VT

Published in the United States by Whisk(e)y Tit: www.whiskeytit.com. If you wish to use or reproduce all or part of this book for any means, please let the author and publisher know. You're pretty much required to, legally.

ISBN 978-1-952600-15-9

For Rye, Rak, Day, Aguirre, & Wetzler.

Thank y'all for nodding along.

*…I know not why matter should be
unworthy of divine nature…*

—Spinoza

Zigong asked, 'What do you think of me?'
'You are a vessel.'
'What kind of vessel?'
*'A vessel that holds offerings of sorghum and
millet*
in the ancestral temple.'

—The Analects of Confucius, 5.4

Contents

Preface

The Hagiography of a Disc Jockey is an undiscovered text. All extant evidence for its existence is compiled here in this volume. It seems apparent to us that the authors of these texts share little knowledge of each other's individual projects, though they all discourse on aspects of the same object. What we have here is apocrypha without canon. If the *Hagiography* can be conceptualized as an unknown and unmeasured three-dimensional object, then these collected works are two-dimensional planes slicing through it—intersecting at their points of agreement and running parallel across their contradictions, all covering different registers of narrativized space. Present here are all the problems of discovered texts. Lacunae abound. We've done our best to piece the parts into discrete wholes, shake the foundation of its sand. The world revealed by these scribes has yet to be fully unearthed but is by all evidence unquestionably real.

1

Mendicant

"Good?"

Eyes rise to Cliff packing a piece in his dugout. Will smiles. The hot pain in his ears hardens at his cheeks' peaking. "Yeah, good."

"Good." Leans against the alley wall. Mural run to grimy smudge blooming behind him. The air fills with pissy grass. An exhale. Ash-and-resin clod knocked, Cliff makes to pass the pipe and box. "Need?"

"Nah, I'm fine." All swallowed. Teeth tight. Jaw clenched. Tongue stiff and swole up and aching.

"You sure? Look like you've had a long one."

"Mmhmm, yeah." Cigarette smoke hits Will's throat like cool lead, lungs like pebbles. Menthol's got nothing to offer the stony agony. Set to sprawl at the crest of the lunch rush—a scratchy throat and thumbtacks in his ears.

"How many doubles've you worked this week, Willie?"

Three fingers.

"All in a row."

Nods.

"Off tomorrow?"

Shakes his head. Can't tell if the heat rising around his eyes is sweat or tears. Knows everything gets blurry. Nose twists to sniff it away but his sinuses are filled with concrete. Coughs one from way deep.

"Gahdamn, Lee. You sign up for that or Travis botching your schedule on purpose?"

"Need the money." Voice like a brush fire.

Cliff kicks and sits on the upturned milkcrate next to Will's. Unzips his backpack. Removes his knife bag and apron and work shoes, rummages in the remaining mass of cloth, wire, and crumpled paystubs for his own smokes. Not even got his non-slips on yet. Showed up wearing cowboy boots, raw denim jeans, and a bomber jacket—likes to make it clear as dawn after a night too long that the kitchen's failures have amounted ultimately to *his* being inconvenienced.

4

"You know, everyone always needs the money, but hell, son. Unless you've got eviction notices or the law after you, or alimony or some shit like that, best not worry too much about it. Not when you've got family like this." Claps his hand on the back of Will's neck and squeezes—one of his constant paternalisms, commiserative and terrifying.

Will appreciates it. The kitchen here was his first gig after getting chewed up and spat out in twitchy little bits by the University at the end of last year's spring semester. Took all summer to get into the kitchen's rhythms, get the menu memorized top-to-bottom enough to sling without thinking. He was just starting to *feel* it when the autumn semester tumbled in and brought back all the hellish particularities of suburbia. He folded within a month. A panic attack paralyzed him at the grill. Tale as old as they come. Cliff'd been called in that night as well. A three-piece suit, charcoal-gray vest and tie and everything, cufflinks sparkling, looking fresh out the cleaners with his hair slicked, smelling like cologne and pomade. Levelled it all master mason:

"What's the problem?"

"Nothing, Cliff. Just taking a breather. You didn't need to—" And Will kicked the alley's ash bucket over a scootch to hide the spatter of yellow vomit on the concrete. "Just taking a—"

"Busy?"

"Oh yeah, yeah. Wild."

"Just you?" Cliff produced the dugout from his vest's watchpocket.

"Nah, nah. Rory's in too."

"Oh, so just Rory then?"

Point taken. Couldn't muster much else to say. Easy enough to predict where the conversation was going: a back-and-forth cornering Will into accepting the simple diagnosis that he just wasn't slinging fast enough, no moral or essential failing, just not moving with enough giddy-up, something anybody can correct, so go correct it—tickets can only ever come too quick for one cook, but there's always two in the evenings, always backup, never alone, and now, pocketing the dugout, "There's three." Since then, end of last September, Will's been designated dish-bitch on busy nights, occasionally called up to the line to prep on-the-fly or to the salad station to wrangle with the wilted when the shit gets dicey.

"Rory still here?" Cliff asks and drags.

"Nah." Rory'd run off about an hour ago, freaked out after throwing brushfuls of melted butter at the broiler flames, sending wicked, soot-edged tongues licking up to the hood racks—one line of blow too many attempting to offset the comedown of last night's molly. Not the first time. Not the last. Will coughs again. Hacks up a nugget come dislodged from the roiling rock in his head.

"Then who's in the kitchen, Lee?"

"Trav." Will makes to take a puff, but the cherry has fallen.

Cliff smiles and passes his pack over. "Have another. Do the bastard some good to be in it for real for a while." And again with the hand and neck. Another squeeze in the sweat gathered there and, "You're hotter than a motherfucker, you know that? Like boiling."

"Yeah. I think the vents are fucked." Smoke lit out of obligation. Inhale a fist.

"Nah, nah, nah," Rubs his callused palm through the sop, "that's fever shit, Willie. Here." Grabs Will's chin and swivels his head—a nut rusted onto its bolt, coming away in squeals and flakes. Brushes away the slick strings of hair and presses palm to forehead. "Oh, shit yeah, you're on fucking fire."

Will swallows a desert-and-a-half, "I can't go home yet, I need the—"

"Oh, no way dude. No way am I working with

Travis alone." Perches the cig in the corner of his mouth and bends to slough boot from sock. "We'll break it over the fryers."

&

A bead gathers, glitters, globes, and falls into the frazzle of fryer grease and crinkling chicken wing. Will's teetering on the balls of his feet, wracking the mud of his mind trying to remember how long each dozen has been dropped and resisting the urge to surrender and collapse under the weight of the heat. Feels like he's breathing through a straw, like his lungs are full of melted plastic, like someone large and unwashed is sitting their whole hairy weight on his face. Inescapable and dizzying, but Cliff'd assured him 'a couple hours in the schvitz and you'll feel right as ever. It'll be hell, but come closing you'll never feel better. Never had an illness the shit couldn't fix,' so there's a hopeful horizon; a white star setting, bringing blue to bruise black to boil pitch, a convalescent promise. Ache and shiver.

In the peripheral dark, everything continues. Fryer oil pops and spatters. Wings shrivel and rise. Ticket printer hums and clicks a tear-away slice. Another dozen at half price. The air is shredded guitar and grinding vocals, Cliff shrieking alongside perpetually a syllable behind. Rock fist a spatula as the Bluetooth speaker peaks around a falsetto soaring over crags of dissonant riff and roiling double-kick. Bright brinkling shatter of porcelain from the dish-pit.

Travis shouts: "Motherfucking wing night of all nights! Motherfucking—" Releasing the valve on his anger in the fashion of all fed-up line cooks, another plate collides unseen with sink or machine, floor or fixture. Grease and blood are quick to become one. "I can't fucking believe this shit!" Been saying it all day. Finding himself sequestered in the pit and relegated to bitch by a kitchen manager batting clean-up only added to his already present muffin-fisted frustration. "Can *you* fucking believe this shit?" At the start of his floor shift, thrusting his phone's screen into Will's face.

Blade slipped off a tomato's curve and, "Jesus, Trav! I'm trying to, damn near cut my—"

"Sorry, kid. But I just have to, I mean look at this shit."

Will put the knife down and rolled off his gloves to take the phone. There, beneath a mesh of thumbprint and pearlescent schmutz, was an image of a hazel eye blackened by bloodshot whites and conjuncted with boogery gunk. Will cleared his throat and swallowed against the daggering pain heavy in his ears. "The hell am I looking at, Travis?"

"Brynn, man. Brynn sent this to me. Calling out sick. Says she's got pink eye."

Will's belly: a flutter, a fall, a shot dove. "Oh yeah?"

"Yeah, but I mean, looks fake, right?"

Will held the phone closer, adjusted the screen's brightness, double-tapped to zoom-out.

"Nah, she literally just sent a picture of the eye. I want to ask her to send one with her face and prove it, right? Cuz if you google pink eye, this is the shit you get. But, last thing I need is her texts from me reading like I'm asking her for pictures of herself. Larry down at the Chimpden just got bawled-out by his owners for something similar, all this hashtag shit. But, man, how do I know it's not—"

With the image brighter, the day's first fevered sweat broke out in earnest. The marble-throated condition he'd been fighting down since coffee and hangover pummeled his heart to kick. The eye was definitely Brynn's—he'd know that iridescence anywhere, encrusted and swelling or otherwise; that caterpillar brow; the freckles high on her cheek, unburied by foundation, still holding the shine of last night's strobing lights and flashing sights.

"It's always the same with these sorostitutes, man."

Travis took the phone back. "Turn twenty-one and they think they can just walk all over you, you know?"

"Mmhmm," throat sudden sandpaper. Rebar in his neck.

"It's wing night too… Fuck!" Phone away. "Just prep-up extra if you can, I guess. I can't worry about the kitchen *and* be down a server, even if it is Brynn." Plucked one of the tomato slices from the puddling pile. Folded and munched, "Bet she's learned her lesson, though. Not many ways to get pink eye, if you know what I mean. Nasty-ass…"

Took a whole shift of singing happy birthday every time she approached the window, running an order or piking a ticket, to convince her to come out with them last night. DJ AdoThaWyfe was hosting the Bottom's Industry Blowout, half-price everything and no cover if you've got a food-handler's.

"It's in the stars, Brynn! The cosmos is calling!" Rory'd shouted as another cacophonous rendition of the tune dwindled.

"Don't they do it like every week?" Brynn unimpaled a handful of tickets and looked over her shoulder—anxious server's tick at a slowing shift, chronic distrust of anything easy.

"Yeah, yeah, but you don't turn twenty-one every week, hon."

Will was elbow-deep in scald and suds while Rory made his case. The roar of the dish machine drowned out most of the litigation at the window, but he wasn't surprised to find in the alley, as Cliff went from door to door checking the locks and alarms, that Brynn was sat on the milkcrate next to Rory, alternating bowl for Juul.

"Ah," Will lit up his smile, "so you *are* coming?"

"Just this once."

The alley door opened. Cliff: "Everyone got everything?"

An affirmative chorus.

"Alright. Alarms're all set. Let's boogie."

They all rose. Rory hollered, "Shotgun!"

So, Cliff's pickup trundled across town, with Brynn and Will in the bed, hugging the wheel-well humps. At a stoplight, Brynn crawled across the dirt-dusted metal floor, hands-and-knees, to reposition herself on Will's side of the carriage, between him and the chrome toolbox.

"Good?"

She nodded. Smiled. Said: "So high. So, so high." And her nose scrunched to collapse her face into a giggle fit that lasted until they parked a few blocks from the Bottom.

At the top of the street-side stairwell, where music and smoke and strobe rose from the cellar's door, Rory asked, "Where did you go to celebrate last weekend?"

"Oh, we went to Rook's and the Chimpden and—"

"Get ready for something completely different," Will added and ventured a palm to the small of her back, begging her a step down. Brynn inched in, brought shoulder to shoulder.

And such was the night—inching until they found themselves as close as physically possible. There were few words. The music was loud. Everyone was close to everyone. Wherever a touch alighted to find itself accepted, it settled. The small of Brynn's back became wholly substantial to Will's left hand, his shoulder her cheek. Eventually, on a cigarette break from the dancefloor muck, each finger found its counterpart. Another drink, back into the heat, and hands foundered upon hips, neck, hair, and finally lips together, teeth and tongue, and an hour before dawn they fell into her bed, discovered their bodies started closer than they'd imagined. They moved on each other in the manner they'd already played out in curious moments alone that'd left them shamefaced at their ceilings. What was firm and what was soft, where the other's voice hid, what made them all a sudden yipping animal spilled from the moments in surprised stutters and grinding halts. Through the haze, around the edge of the spin, in the dearth of words they didn't think they'd have to cultivate they found more of what they wished to hide of themselves—tufts, sumps, knobs, knots, and burbling...

Morning hit fist-to-face. Sudden light and headache. Will sat up, rubbed his eyes, questioned the night. Lungs tar-tight, joints aching, stomach shredded, sniffles, shaky. Took stock of this new room. Hadn't had much chance to notice anything about it earlier other than that it was huge right before the lights flicked off. Still big in the cruel morning. Massive compared to his hovel southside of town—a studio appended to a fuller-sized house; single-car garage converted into lodgings. Her bed was big too, large enough that when Will fell back into the sheets he did so without collision or contact at all with Brynn's body. She was curled fetal at the edge of the other side. Will reached across the linen expanse, hooked his left arm around her midsection, and pulled her to his chest. Her shoulders rose as sleep took him back to bilious black. When the alarm woke

14

him for work an hour-and-a-half later, Brynn had repositioned herself at the bed's edge. Like to fall off.

"Fuh-uh-uh-uck! I can't goddamn believe this shit!" Another shattering cuts through the kitchen din. "God-fucking-dammit!"

"Everything alright back there, sweetheart?" Cliff readjusts his bandana.

"No. Fuck."

"What's the problem?"

"I got, fuck, I got fucking hot sauce in my, in my eye!"

"Oh, rub some dirt in it. We're almost out of here."

"No, fuck this! I don't get paid to deal with this shit anymore!"

Cliff disappears to the pit. Will leans over the mercifully empty fryers, pressing his forehead to the greasy, hot shelf. Sweat's pouring now. Tunnel-vision. Nose running. All of it falling drop after globby drop into the fry oil. Sputs and bubbles before sinking in clots to tumble around the submerged heating element. There are chippies across the Atlantic that pride themselves on never having changed their oil. Most of the questions on the food handler's exam are about how hot stuff needs to be to kill everything in it enough to eat. Will closes his eyes and tries to ignore that he can hardly breathe.

"Hey! Hey! Woah, woah!" And a hand again again on the back of his neck. "Don't you go falling in!"

Eyes rise to Cliff standing over him, holding him up.

"Good?"

"Nuh-uh, no…"

"Good."

&

Wash water chills to poultrescent slime on Will's forearms. Everything now, shiver at his cheeks, is set free to flow by fever's breaking levee. A hollow fills him. A void sheathed in prickling skin. Smoke still fits like a foot in his throat, but the scorching has subsided. Now there's only the swell. Only the nausea's shift, like he'd spent the day at sea. His eyes are full of sand. He's hungry.

The alley door opens, and Cliff joins him. Takes his crate. Packs his piece and passes it over.

"Nah, I don't think I—"

"Last step. Set you right." Reaches to pluck the cigarette from Will's mouth. Replaces it with the cool metal irony of the one-hitter's butt. "Hit that. Get you some nosh. I'll make a quick cheeseburger before we split. Have a beer. You'll be right as—" Fire flicks.

Will moves his face and the piece's pack away from the flame. "I definitely shouldn't drink tonight, Cliff. That sounds like a terrible—"

"You definitely shouldn't drink *tomorrow*, but you're on a hell of a comedown. Gonna need the dog's hair if you want to stabilize. Kicked whatever bug you had, but there's a deeper condition that needs tending to." Flicks again. "Hit it."

Resinous crackle and the smoke coils in the cavern. Rolls its scales against the raw flesh of Will's scooped innards, bites at all the soft scurrying in the dark. Itch and tumble, he holds his breath against the slither.

"Good?"

"Mmhmm."

She was new. First day, insofar as he was aware—so: "That's bullshit."

Leaning against the wall, holding a Juul at her bottom lip, staring at the mural.

Will took his crate. Kicked the other across the concrete, "Sit. Sit if you're on break."

"I'm not on break."

"I know. You should sit." Her face: raw panic. Eyes like broken windows. "Sit down. Sit down."

She sat. A whispering pull from her Juul.

"You want a real cigarette? You look like you could use a real cigarette."

"Ok."

"This is a terrible place to hide, you know. First place managers'll look for you is in the alley. Bust you for smoking too much—"

"I'm not hiding."

Will smiled and straightened his posture. "You're definitely trying to, though. Don't sweat it. Shit sucks. Fuck the customers, they don't know anything." Platitudes laid-out flat. "Your only real job is to take their money, you know? Highway robbery. Up-sell, up-sell, up-sell. Slip in automatic gratuity if they're giving you shit. Think about it like that and you'll be able to deal with a lot more than you think."

She smiled. A dainty toke. Not yet a smoker. First shift, for sure.

"But, again, alley is a terrible place to hide. You want to for real for real get out the shit, grab a bus bin and bring it to the dish-pit in back of the kitchen—"

"Travis said that servers should stay out of the—"

"Travis says a lot and it's all bull. Cliff makes the real rules. Don't get it twisted."

Every fifteen minutes it seemed like—busy or slow, didn't matter—she'd come to the back of the kitchen hefting one of the grimy black bins pressed against her aproned hips. Didn't seem to bother her when they were full, but she'd never allow their emptiness

18

to excuse her from making the trip. She'd bring bins back sloshing and clattering with nothing but drink-swill and stray glimmers of silverware, or even bring them totally empty, say they 'need a little rinse' and slide up next to him at the sinks, grabbing the hose herself. Jet to blast crud and scuzz from the plastic. A few weeks at most had passed before, on one of Will's chronic doubled-doubles, she brought back a cup of coffee.

"Look like you could use a boost."

"Oh, wow. Thanks, B!" First time he let slip the sobriquet.

"No problem, Lee. I don't know how you take it, but I can run you some milk or sugar or half-and—"

"No, no. Black is fine."

"Ok, cool. Uhm…" And she looked around. No bin, no tarrying alibi.

"Chill, Brynn. Chill. Take a minute. Travis or Cliff won't get caught dead in the dish-pit, they'll get like PTSD or something. Relax."

And an exhale drags its nails across the newly burst pustules and carbuncles in his throat. Furious hacks. Globs of whatever filth had caked follow up the smoke, tonsil stones thrown and phlegm flying. An animal sound from somewhere deep and numb, near a growl. Tears take the sand from his eyes and his nose runs fresh. Tannic tinge about his teeth. A dry heave. Immaculate, hollow, full-up with hefty nothing—

"Good?"

"Mmhmm." Will sits up, body plumbed perfectly leaden and inert. Grins—the corners of his mouth taken upward by the blissy rise behind his eyes.

"Good."

2

Pleasance

"Love you too—" and the phone clatters to bathroom tile. Head back to knees. Slime of a cold sweat. A tumble. Belly voids.

Pip, pulp, and pith leave quivering husk. Somewhere in the empty there still churns a curdle, something all a quease begging to slough. Clung fast and climbing.

Eyes sealed by salt and cheek stiff in agony. A hand in the pain-wrought dark grabs the rim of the wastepaper basket beneath the toilet roll. Drags it over. Can hear it. Can smell what's spilled. Can't see anything, but would've known that tremble anywhere:

"—well, Brynnie-bee, we're just proud is all of the

woman you've become," never been able to look us in the eye without tears breaking up over his, not since our early-teens at least. Proud of the woman we've become but still become a woman. Daughter and the rest of it. Could never quite bear to recognize anything other than "the drive and ambition you have and of the, well, I reckon just about all of it is all. Hope school's not getting you down and working isn't pushing you too hard and you've still got your, uhm, well, still got your eyes on the prize as they and all just to say I guess that I love you, your Mama loves you, and happy birthday again from the bottom of my heart, sugar. We love you."

Then: That that'd been holding it all together gave its first giving way.

Now: Head in the plastic bin. What's left for the body to rid itself of comes up. Claws. Ropes of glass. Stalactite. Flush.

Wonder if they can hear. No doubt they're already up. Early afternoon on a weekday. They've got classes though so maybe, but Sasha'll be sat at the nook like always. Books stacked to one side, phone in front of her. No headphones. Scrolling through Insta. Peaky, garbled video snippets erupting into the quiet of the kitchen, and you'll get a clementine from the fridge to have something to look at, to have something to do with your shaking hands because she'll be posted up there procrastinating all day just to get the question in and twisted between your ribs: "So, who is he?"

And you'll have to say "Who?" Roll the fruit round in your palms. Always juicier once it's bruised inside. Make it look mindless, routine, like you aren't already sweating again.

"That's what I'm asking you, B." She'll say something like that probably, something almost rehearsed because she'll be sat there all morning waiting for your shameful descent down the stairs, your desperate breakfast, all to catch you with the reminder that, "Hey, I don't care. Taylor comes over all the time. None of the other girls care either, I bet—" But you'd all still made it a point to make it a point when you moved in together end of last summer that once the semester was underway, once you all got serious because being this close to finished is being just as close to starting at all having been the biggest mistake of your lives, that there weren't going to be any boys allowed during the week because you all could already tell that that just wasn't going to fly but she'll bet, "That none of them even noticed."

"Then how did you know, Sash?"

"Oh," And she'll grin, stick out her tongue, bite behind the stud, cross her eyes and say something probably like, "Well, Taylor and I definitely heard you. Didn't quite get a good look at—" or maybe she'll drop "I was here when he left, having breakfast. Looked like a stray-dog brought inside just for a beating," but not that exactly because that's something like what Papa'd say.

And the clementine's skin'll have come away, fiddling right off itself. What little appetite you might muster will have been kicked and stomped to dust and the nausea will most likely rise again as you look at the opened fruit, so very much like something killed and still living. Body cleared of consequence, the night again has room to bloom. Dripping neon in the hounded head's hollow catches on half remembered shoulders. Hands and everything else. Inseparable mass of everyone in that basement bar's dinge and din. The music returns with blood's passage no longer plaqued sludgy. Panic. Tune of the drum and only the drum drumming until there's nothing but sudden reverberant liquor-slick flesh and begging under it all to wait, stop, take a breath to lock hands in the cool night, dewfall mingling with the sweat and finally a kiss and the shower curtain hisses across its rod. Crank the faucet's knob. Pull the plunger to send it up and back to scorch and pelt. To curl fetal in the basin.

Amniotic wash returns the body to self. Lay there where the steam rises from, below the cloud. Water gathering around, pooling in elbowed nooks and hamstrung dams, streams with a dark tinge away from skin. Carries off his hands firstly. Thumbed grime piled in the places he'd grabbed the most, all rote as the morning rose. Waist and the softening of jaw. Left breast lovelessly pressed and pinched. Bruises yet unburgeoned on thighs where his palms plied the laze and ride. Nothing all that willing to rise. All always slipping out and then he'd apologize, mumble, groan, grope, and say something he didn't mean and might not remember. Stops started, halts and fondly ceasings, grumble and collapse.

Hands fold prayerful between legs. The only place yet untouched on the water's way. Touched now.

"You shouldn't be blushing, hon," Sasha'll say as you muscle a wedge past your teeth, "there's no shame in this household. Not the environment we all came together to create—" Still sounds like Papa, though, those declarations like that. Not how she would say it. Would be more along the lines of like "No worries, B. Get what you gotta get when you need to get it," maybe. Then she'll pry as to how it was, a play-by-play, and you'll have to say that you have to admit that you really don't remember, and the clementine's juices, perhaps out of season and not as ripe as you'd like, will wash over your smoke-numb tongue like the scummy waters of low-tide and your knees will go weak and hands start to tingle and the only seat available will be the nook's outer bench and so you'll sit and stare down at the fruit's gaping wound and all the sweet will turn sour and Sasha'll go on and on and on: "Wild nights for a while after your twenty-first. Remember mine? Don't be so, don't be so down on yourself. Not a mistake unless you let it become one. Just one night. Just one night where you took yourself out and got what you wanted and now, rest up of course, but now you can just, you know, take a minute and you been so hard on yourself and, hon, the semester's almost over and this isn't even a real slip up. Got what you wanted right? Got some guy over here to blow your back out and, shit, ain' nothing to worry over, you didn't fuck up for nothing. Take the day, recover. Remember what you can, and smile about it. Life's too short to get bent out of shape over rules that we all agreed upon together so just let it go. No one really cares but you, so you've got to decide what it is that you need to do. You know what I mean, sugar? You went and got yours, got what you wanted, so be happy. Check it off the list, Brynnie-bee. Do whatever you want, honey-bear, so long as it's whatever you want," but Sasha doesn't call you Brynnie-bee or honey-bear or anything like that. That's what Papa calls us and Papa didn't say anything like what Sasha'll say. Papa just called to "Beg to differ, little miss! You've seen the footage, we've all seen the footage."

Could hear him rise through the line. Machinery of his chair back home squealing and clapping as the footrest came down. Standing to pace and make his case, recount the evidence found on that warbly VHS tape. Eleven years of good-humored deliberation. "You stood there at that sink and washed off all that work what your Mama'd done painting stars and hearts and whatever else a fairy's got on her face to make her out a fairy, washed it all off with that deadly serious look, got your dress all—"

"Gown," we said.

"*Gown*, apologies, your majesty." Could hear him smiling. Just about wide enough to break the seal and get his eyes welling. "Got it all over that dress though, didn't you? Stood there and I come in with the camera and said what in all hell and you just, you just frowned at me and said to me like I was the one being silly that, you said Papa fairies ain' real and I'm too grown-up for magic and—"

"I did not!" Our wrist came up to smother a giggle.

27

A sniff the smell of rubber, bleach, the sea. Condom still dangling between our fingers. A dry wretch. Belly reminded of its bitter.

"Oh, you did too! Looked me right in the eye like I was a fool for thinking you a fairy!"

"And you made me wear that dress—"

"*Gown*, sugar, it was a gown because you were a *princess*."

Sour joy. "You guys made me wear it out trick-or-treating even though it was all covered in face-paint and all wet and—"

"You tried to make me carry your candy around for you, too!"

"Well, I was *still* a princess, so…"

"Oh, hush up."

"Mama didn't throw that one away? It was ruined."

"Course she didn't throw it away. She made it for you and, she's kept all of them. Same dress, *gown*, same gown every year for who knows how long. Amazing to look at 'em, Brynnie-bee, next you're back home you'll have to take a look, all laid out like she had 'em. Easy to forget how little you used to be. Amazing to see how much you grew every year and how much well—" all of it to say, to just remind us that they haven't been doing nothing, or don't want us to think that they've been doing nothing but "Sitting around and missing you."

Never less present, though, than under him. Not even a place where he was happening, this kitchen boy. Untruffled duff beneath the boar, turned up, over, and out nonetheless and bare all the more. Touched now. Precious as a pearl, hard away in its inert mothering shell. Not until it must be, and then by then all dead and broken in shards well on their way to weathering down toward sand. Sediment. Up from so much dust. Obliging and unfussed over. Free and unfelt for all the noxious thrum making so much more the less. A foundering there and not an ought in sight. Pleasurelessly plural. Nothing between. Nothing mystic. No third thing formed from wholes rendered halves. Simple not. Bliss beneath his failing. His eyes, liquor-locked and glassy, terrarium dead, stared not through to the bed beneath but instead as if there was nothing at all under him to see.

Knees now to chest. Charlie-horses grinding hooves. Toes curling. Tendons tight. Fingers hooked in every place possible and, from the inside this time, a boom of ecstatic absence.

Shaking into stillness. Breathing. Only breathing. Everything still, save the breath. The deepest substance, life on lung.

Sinuses run in the steam. Tears in full. Trickle back. Pleasance.

On our neck as he rose to finally leave: Beer, smoke, sweat, and ourselves all spread hanging in his beard. Belly flipped at the kiss on our cheek.

"Oh, well, hon, didn't mean to, uhm, if it's your usual thing to sleep-in when you, don't let me be the one keeping you from—"

"No, no. We should get up. I should get up. I need to, uhm…" Shifting then on the bed, readying ourselves, the fluff-crusted shuck of something stuck peeled from our inner thigh. Flicked the comforter away and opened our legs to find the shriveled slime of a condom shining out pallid against our groin's doughsome blush.

"You ok, Brynnie? I think you maybe cut-out or—"

"No, yeah. I'm fine." Held it up to the light. Flocculate gathered at the bell's-end reservoir. Pubic corkscrews and crusty pills like an eraser furied over a guess etched dark and indelible. "Just waking up, Papa. Still got a head full of sand."

"Well, again, I'm sorry to have woke you. Just wanted to get my happy birthday in and—"

"Thanks Daddy, I appreciate it. It's been, it was

a long celebration. So I think I'm just, it's all just catching up to me is all."

"Oh, I'm sure I understand. Just hope it was a *good* long celebration and ain' done too much to set you behind or none."

Standing then: a cold scurry. A clump of whatever was poured out last night descended and plopped to the carpet. "It was fine, I suppose. Nothing to write home about. The usual, uhm, the usual." Palm pressed. A finger. All tack and flake and, deeper, trembling sop. We muttered: "Fuck…"

"What's that, Brynnie?"

"Nothing. Nothing."

"Alright. Well, I don't know much else, hon. Mama said she's gonna try and call you before dinnertime or after Bible study tonight so if you're around then—"

"I've, uhm," Looked down from our window onto the busying street below. Flower petals from the early blossoms, already blown and spated to withering by April cloudbursts, stuck to the sidewalk, piling at the grassy edges, a jammy path cut by joggers and dogs and all other manner of footfall and, "I've got work tonight so, I won't be, uhm, class tomorrow too actually, so—"

"Fuck that shit." Sasha'll say. "Take a day. Call in

sick. Tell them you've got pink eye or something. Fuck that shit." And the clementine'll be rent to bits. Pooling and mashed. Uneaten. Under your fingernails. Hands sticky. It'll be all you can smell, all you can taste, all there is because in another fifteen minutes the water is going to run cold.

3

Tonsure

"C'mon, get in the truck." Cliff's hand on Rory's moonlit shoulder, cutoff sleeve and tufted flesh. Clean smell of foliage in the night, sliced through with the onion and copper effulgence of fear and blood. A tacky crust gives and crumbles at the press of Cliff's palm, something like mud.

"Did you, man, did you call a cops on me?" Rory's sway switches to a step away, back toward the sheltering shadow of early spring overgrowth, verdure violet in the night.

"No, I didn't call the cops on you, Ror. Get in the truck." Cliff's grip shifts. Kind and palmy slips to firm and guiding. Index and thumb now plied tight to the back of Rory's neck. "You're lucky I saw you. Lucky I *recognized* you."

Tattered forms akin to Rory's are not uncommonly found along this stretch of state roadway, between the city limits and the manicured bosk of Grouseland State Park. Marching equally sparse at all hours, single or in pairs, they are the more intrepid of the county's unhoused population. Any given local motorist will have seen them often enough to blow past without a second thought.

Rory is "Damn lucky," Cliff reminds and relaxes his hold.

Rory stops. Digs his non-slips into the roadside gravel. "Hey man, you can't call the cops on me, man. Just like—"

"No one is calling the cops, Ror. Just get in the truck."

"Who the fuck is calling the, are you gonna call the fucking cops?"

Cliff presses in hard again, but the mix of sweat and dew and all the slippery rest gives him only the shirt to grab when Rory bolts.

Collar in hand. Throaty shred of wet fabric tearing. Muddy thud as Rory eats it into the drainage ditch.

Takes Rory a second to rise from where he's fallen, a second longer to get his balance on the slope. Turns to look back at Cliff, now sparking up his last cigarette. Makes no gesture of recognition. Walks toward the woods.

The entirety of the forest along this vein of road is penned-in by chicken-wire fencing. Difficult to see in the daylight for the vines and grass, impossible at this hour for the lampless dark. There're only a few places where the fence has been collapsed, stomped down for ease of entry by the transients seeking sanctuary in nature's baroque savagery.

By the time Cliff has smoked his last to the filter, Rory's either given up or forgotten himself altogether. A few too many briary handfuls. Now still at the edge of the forest, leaning to fall before jerking back upright.

Cliff flicks his butt onto the asphalt and offers a kinder gambit than before, doing his level best to keep the edge out of his voice: "Hey! You need a ride, buddy?"

Rory looks over his shoulder, then back into the trees.

&

House is too damn big. Only ever feels it when he's for some reason got to be awake through the night.

Usually after blowing off some post-work steam, obliging beer-and-shot specials, Cliff'll roll up the gravel drive, beeline for a shower, and go to bed, wet and dripping; sleep a whole day away if he's got one to spare, otherwise it's rise-shine-and-boogie back into town to work the restaurant, reassembling the kitchen from its perpetual shambles. Never gets much chance to see the whole house for too long. Forgets there's still three or four rooms totally unfurnished, still smelling like dust and sundried mildew. A bathroom in the basement he's never used, dining room with no table. He'd put the floors in himself though, tore up the carpet and everything years ago.

"Nice place," Rory says rounding the corner into the kitchen. It's nearly three in the afternoon.

"Good morning," Cliff tops the sandwich he'd been in the process of making. "How're we feeling?"

"I think I'll be alright." Rory leans against the counter. Still in nothing but boxers, still holding the wad of blood gunked paper towel against the left side of his face.

"Careful with that bandage there." Cliff turns to his coffee machine. Had a pot in the night, made a fresher one after sunrise, kept it warming all day for when or if Rory finally woke.

Presses his palm. Hisses through his teeth. "The hell happened?"

"Not a clue, man. I found you like this on the side of the fucking road." Places a steaming mug on the counter. "Had to drag you into the house. Slumped unconscious once you were sat in the truck. Carried you like you're my wife, slung over my arms, cradled, keep the mud off the floors. Sat you up on the toilet. Slapped you awake and—"

"Goddamn."

"Yeah man. Don't remember anything?"

"Not a lick. Remember going to the Bottom with you and Willie and, was Brynn with us?"

"Yeah brother, but that was like three days ago almost."

"Fuck me," Rory raises the mug to his lips and sips. A scalding dribble falls down his chin and hits his belly. "Shit!" Spills a blat to the floor. "God, fuck, shit!"

Cliff produces a rag from a drawer close at hand and throws it down. Stomps it onto the tile before the coffee can stain the grout.

"Sorry man." Wipes his mouth. "Where's, uhm, where's my clothes at?"

"Trashed them. You were covered head to foot in mud and blood and who the hell knows what else."

"Goddamn."

Cliff, in his attempt to hold Rory upright enough to wake, had torn the t-shirt the rest of the way to shreds. Figured then that he might as well do away with delicacy altogether. He'd set to shucking shoes and socks. Chef's pants had a gaping hole in the crotch. Uncinched and pulled down, something horrible. Unwashed briefs came off like chicken skin, revealing pimple-shocked flesh. Cliff fought a gag and purge. To have blown chunks over an AWOL line-cook's twig-and-berries would have been a fall too far. He stood then to collect himself before turning on the shower. Kept it cold, see if it'd jolt Rory back to consciousness. It did. Briefly:

Eyes blasted open. Gasping. Whole body went stiff. Fright-charged arms pushed Cliff away and the rest of Rory fought with the curtain. A few jerks and kicks and then his feet came out from under him, and he fell backwards into the tub. Conked out again. Something on the way down reopened the gash on the left side of his head. The water ran thick and red.

Did the best there was to do stanching the flow. Head wounds always look worse than they actually are so he stayed calm, ran the water warmer, and washed him by hand. It's never what's pouring out of the head that's worth the worry, it's what's been shaken up inside.

"Let's have a look again here," Cliff says a few bites into his sandwich. "Turn your head, let me see." Grabs Rory by the chin and twists. "Hurt?"

"Yeah."

"Dizzy at all?"

"I don't know. I feel like I got hit by a fucking bus."

"You may have. You very well may have." Cliff pinches the amassment of paper towel by something approximating a corner and lifts. Foil torn from yogurt and the wound's morass materializes. Impossible to read without a trained eye whether its initial opening had been by blunt force or laceration or whatever else, but obvious to the blind that the damn thing is "Bleeding again, shit. Shit."

Cliff reopens the drawer and produces another rag. Rips the failing paper towel from Rory's head and replaces it.

"Hold that and, uhm," bloody dimes fall from the ridge of Rory's chin, collect as loose change on the "Goddamn tile, shit. Fuck. Uhm, close your eyes Rory, don't want you to—"

He's already swaying.

"Rory, Rory, hey bud, can you open your eyes?" Cliff guides him down by the armpits, sits him on the floor. Rory's eyes roll over white, lips green blue. "C'mon man, give me something."

Eyes open. Dripping crystal slits.

"Hey, hey, hey. We're going to get you to the hospital, alright? Get this whole thing stitched up. You're going to be—"

"Nah, nah, I can't. I can't, don't have the fucking, uhm, I'm fine, I'm fine. Just let me—"

&

Four days:

"A good place to dry out, if nothing else."

"Certainly is," and Rory thrusts a borrowed boot into the side of a rotting log. Patches of emerald moss and several brass-band's worth of trumpeting mushrooms.

Cliff stops. Makes a show of breathing. "Can't find air like this in town, you know? Even though it's a small place, still reeks of city. Gasoline, cigarettes, trash moldering. People. You know what I mean?"

Rory removes the toe from the hole he's made. Compost spills to soil.

"You ever get out to Grouseland?"

Worming grubs and the skitter of some shiny, black, terrified mass. "Not in a long time."

40

"It's nice." Cliff puts his hands on his hips. "Not like this, though. Grouseland's got all those trails and shit, signs and guideposts and all that. This is, this here is like real, actually wilderness basically."

Rory squints. Trees and dirt and leaves. Something out here is poison, something surprisingly edible; something older than the country itself, something so new it may as well be dead. All the same in the end maybe. He turns to look back. They've not yet gone deep enough for the forest behind them to swallow where they'd come from. The hard geometry of Cliff's house cuts through the arboreal mesh. *Real, actually wilderness basically.* Almost.

As Rory looks back ahead into the evering pathlessness before them Cliff steps in close, pinchy fingers reaching for the now neater dressing over his wound.

"Don't flinch. Let me take a look."

Four days of paternal pestering:

"No, no, no, lay back down. Lay back down. Rest up." Cliff'd say bringing Rory another glass of water, another warm, drippy rag, another aspirin.

"It's ok, it's ok," He'd coo pouring a sizzling dram of hydrogen-peroxide over the moist mush of weepy, fleshen sump.

"Don't pick," he'd chide every single time he walked by.

Four days laid up under Cliff's cloying care. Four days poked and prodded and poured over like an ancient manuscript while the wound festered, swelling to stiffen and lock his jaw. Four days of being helplessly cleaned and preened and fawned over while within, wound aside, demons clawed and kicked and snarled their hunger against his soul's soft shell. He'd no idea which agony rose from which source, which specific substance each ache was calling out for. Chills gave over to feverish sweats and sleep eluded him; though that did little to stop the nightmares materializing. Dark figures, eyeless shadows, stood still in his peripherals, disappearing every time he tried to catch them reaching. On the second day he'd lost control of his bladder and bowels. Luckily, since he'd been unable to eat for lack of appetite for anything but nameless numbing agents and pills of bliss, as well as his jaw's tooth-grinding clench, he'd had nothing in him to void but water and electrolyte solution. All that he'd spilled to soil himself was diamond-clear piss and tacky sludge smelling of all death boiled down to a weapons-grade concentration. He'd tried to vomit at the smell, but it gathered behind a fortification of tooth and tongue, came in fiery phlegmatic jets from his nose. Mingled with tears. When Cliff arrived from work that night, he'd again wordlessly carried Rory cradled to the shower, undressed him, and washed him of his filth by hand without so much as a glint of disapproval in his eye.

"Just gotta be diligent about infection, you know?" Unsticks a strip of adhesive holding the gauze on. Cliff'd watched a few field dressing tutorials on his phone in the kitchen during the slump between the lunch and dinner rushes. Got it pretty well practiced at this point. "Gets infected and I'm gonna have to take you to the hospital, dig?"

"I know," Rory growls. Still talking exclusively from the right-side of his mouth. "I know."

The bandage comes away and the cool of the air whispers kindly against the skin and rent flesh. It stings, but no longer in the way of a vampire thrust into sunlight. Where the wound once wept, it now sighs. The sides are puckering, islanding a scab in new, pink scar tissue. It's deep. Long time before it won't be a worry. Cliff'd assured him at every opportunity: 'Stay as you need. I'll cover your kitchen shifts until this stops being a blatant health-code violation, then you can come on back. Until then you're welcome to stay here.'

43

"Looks to be drying-up nicely." Cliff re-engages the adhesive strip with Rory's cheek. "Another two weeks tops."

Rory's heart falls.

Cliff steps back away and digs in a pocket for his cigarettes. Lights one. Vegetal musk dispelled by menthol and tar.

"Can I get one?" Rory asks.

"You sure?"

"Yeah, man." Fist balled at his side, "I'm good."

"Alright. Cool, cool."

Cliff does everything for him: perches the butt on the unswollen side of Rory's mouth, lights it up, looks into Rory's eyes as he inhales the first drag. Rory's lips glisten Pavlovian around the filter. On the exhale he turns away and steps over the log he'd been kicking.

The cigarette quiets something, brings a lightness to the fore of Rory's mind. One of the imps that'd been rattling around has been momentarily satisfied. With the quiet comes clarity. For Rory now, stepped separate and away from Cliff's clinging, there is only pain and this forest. Even the house behind has been for the moment forgotten. Pain and the forest and they aren't so different from each other.

"Lucky man, Ror. You know that?"

"Huh?"

A smirk muddies Cliff's face, "It doesn't often happen like this. Don't always come out of this shit unscathed like you're like to be."

An inhale and Rory closes his eyes, squeezes them shut until the searing against his skull forces them back open. Then, as the pain fades, there's the forest. "Yeah, I uhm, I appreciate you being there and here and—"

"Oh, it's nothing, brother. Would have done the same for me, I expect." Steps over the destroyed log.

"I guess that's—"

"What we do for each other, right? That's how it goes. All a family, you know? Gotta keep the kitchen woven tight, all hands on deck, all for one and one for—"

Pain and the forest. Walking now. It's beautiful enough. Tied together, knit tight and balanced but, Rory winks as a tendril of smoke flicks his watering eye.

"—Gotta make sure we've all got each other's backs, you know? That's the core of how the kitchen has got to work, each individual hand put in the service of catching the fall of someone else. Right?"

All the lie because none of this rose for the sake of anything other than itself. Vines don't hold the trees up and the trees don't give the vines something to climb. No. The sun is way up high, right? The sun is way, way up high.

"So that's how like, and you know I know that seems like a lot of pressure to put on you guys. I get that but, that's what's so great about doing it like we do it, woven together and holding everything together for each other, is that there's no way to fuck up, you understand? Because—"

Since the sun is way, way up high and the tree needs to have the sun, then the tree goes way, way up high. The vine, though, needs the sun as well so it climbs the tree but given the opportunity, the tools, the power, it would just as soon chop it down.

"Because man, we'll never let you fall all the way, you understand? I'm not trying to like be like whatever or anything, but just know that I've got your back and you can come to me with anything, dig? Anything, Ror. Been in some dark places myself, should tell you about it sometime, but listen—

So it is with everything beautiful and natural, though. It's all agony, screaming verdant anguish. Even the sloping ground here is part of the battle, trees growing up and against its fall, its obvious will away from the heights, taking the water's rill to fill up the lake. A cycle, a machine of self-renewal, sustainable or whathaveyou, the cogs are keening for relief and relief can only mean collapse and decay. At the bottom all is death. The world piles.

"And just what in fuck's name is all this now!"

As they've been walking a sun-silvered shimmer and cool breeze has risen. Out of the humid, shady mirth comes the lake, Lake Mikal, Grouseland State Park its opposite bank.

"I can't fucking believe this shit!" And Cliff bends in the periphery to inspect a hollow at a tree's roots. A flurry of woodchips and twigs and dirt and there is a great whooshed uncrumpling of something heavy and blue and, "Goddammit. Goddammit. Goddammit."

"What is it?" Rory turns from the shining mass of water, glints carving purples, yellows, and blues into his squinted vision.

"A fucking tarp, like fucking, shit!" Cliff kicks at the duff and leaves and then, clank and shatter, empty 40s, cans of fruit and fish and cat food, a coffee tin filled with ash. "Goddamn bums. Knew it was coming sooner or later but, shit man. Fuckers are everywhere now!"

&

Three weeks:

The kitchen boys have got the close down pat, been pulling their extra weight without so much as a bead of sweat breaking, so Cliff walks out into the alley and lets the door shut behind him. Used to be he'd hang around, have a drink, roll into town, but now he's walking to the parking lot. Going to just go on home.

The house has shrunk up to a proper size with Rory taking up the living room. A mattress where the couch used to be. Clothes piled pyramidic over the proud plain of hardwood floor. Flat screen television in the corner, a gaming console, brand unrecognizable to Cliff, coiled and humming. Usually Rory's laid propped up on an elbow and rolled pillow, screen flashing his shadow all around. It's a far better sight than how he'd been that first week of recovery. Cliff coming home to find him half-asleep, twitching in the dark, screaming himself awake and into cold sweats.

Worst of all was that second day where Rory'd ruined the couch completely. Cliff'd done what he had to and cleaned the kid up. By then Rory's body had softened to show the trauma of his bender's final night in full bloom: Big bruises blotched about his arms and legs, swallowing the shapes of shrapnel-shot tattoos that already covered so much of his skin. His calves were cut up to scabby bits and his feet swollen, toes curved inward, nails cracked and purpling. To even imagine the agony Rory was currently living in, how all-encompassing and ultimately anaesthetizing pain like that can be, was enough to set Cliff sat at the top of an endless, spiraling reverie, legs dangling and dizzy.

Running a rag of darkening suds between Rory's legs and voidfully reeking cheeks, Cliff found himself muttering, mouth sour with the urge to spit, the words: "It's ok, baby. But you've got to stop all this. You've got to stop all this."

And the hand attached to the voice that'd cooed those words to Cliff so many black years back lifted his chin to bring his eyes level with her own. There were no tears to be found on her cheeks, not a twitch of pity. She brought the rag, smelling of his vomit and blood, of garlic and iron and waxen castile, to his eyes to wipe away what quivered and shimmered there as if in truth he by his sins was undeserving of his tears' torrent, as if part of his punishment was to continue holding it all in so that he would know just how much chaos he was meant to set in order, unallowed to lighten his load. He tried then, as she wiped a clot from his lips, to ask "Where's Leah?" but the sibilant combined with the swell of his tongue and muck of his mouth was only enough to knock yet another tooth from its frail hold and sput a spittle pebbled gout down his chin.

"Hush, hush," she'd said. He need not have asked at all. She knew it would be the only question the blended soup of his brain would think to have, guilt bound to push through the mass of mucus and cracked teeth. She answered, "Leah is asleep in her crib. Where she should be. You shouldn't worry about Leah anymore."

The next memory Cliff has is of the room he woke up in days later. Furnished with two cots and kitschy decorative landscape paintings. Windows with bars, filigreed to pretend against their imprisoning. Walls taupe and peach. All somehow just as dark and empty as his mouth. Sandy tongue rolling against bare and cratered gum.

Ran his tongue then over his dentures, licking away the worst of the memory and soundlessly flitting the lateral approximate that fronted his daughter's name. Take for granted that the body thought to run nerve endings into the center of every tooth until most of them have gone missing at the behest of fist and brick. Can't feel a thing. Knows his mouth is closed mostly because he can't get it any more shut. Food numbly runs to mush. A perpetual drooling problem.

The clods of underbaked gunk that Rory'd been shitting snaked longer and cut up with brackish jets of water. No amount of wiping was going to keep anything cleaner than the flow of the shower already was, so Cliff turned Rory round to lean against the wall, hang from the washcloth rack, and let the jet flow off his shoulders, river through his crack. A storm muddied estuary gathering around the drain.

After all that could be done was done, once Rory's knees gave to shaking before ceasing to hold him up at all, Cliff swaddled him tight in dirty towels and a spare fitted sheet, laid him down in his own bed. Hoped that his emptied bowels could hold off another round for a few more hours. Then he made for the truck again, adrenaline at the thought of the kid's innards finding more to rid themselves of chopped through the thicket of exhaustion that had been tightening around his mind. Was planning on doing this in the daylight, making a run to get the kid's stuff so that he'd be more comfortable while he recovered, but Cliff figured if his insides are going to keep trying to become his outsides he'd much prefer Rory ruin material Rory'd paid for himself.

Doesn't reckon now, rolling down the truck's

window, cutting the radio, and lighting up an after-work smoke, that he'd be able to find it again. All in a driven mania, the image of Rory's house and its approximate location materialized in Cliff's mind right alongside the nightmare vision of the kid shitting all over the bed, of the house flooding with the discharge of a failing body. Couldn't remember in the moment whether he'd ever picked Rory up from his own place to drive him to work, or maybe slightly tipsy he'd at some point driven him home after a night out, but Cliff *knew* where he was going. One of the two in some way must be true. All autopilot, blasting back into town and through streets increasingly narrow and potholed until he found a clutter of lodgings that might have once been called townhouses. Cracked windows and trash. Crushed cans and cigarette boxes littering the overgrown yards, glittering foil and cellophane. Again, something like a memory told him where to park despite all the housefronts looking the same. Peered through the main entrance's wire-crossed, shatter-proof window to see a vanilla-lit hallway of numbered apartment doors. One of them had envelopes shoved between the frame and handle. Bold letters marked the fronts. Cliff could make out just enough to know they were notices of eviction.

He tried the main entrance's knob and discovered it locked.

Cliff smiles with his exhale. Cracks his neck. There are some things that once learned are impossible to forget. A back-alley, ball-peen lobotomy couldn't dislodge his knowledge of a B&E's finer techniques. One day he'll be a demented invalid, mumbling perfectly coherent treatises on lock-picking to his grandkids. Getting in was easy. *Being* in that apartment, however...

The thought of it rolls his stomach now, menthol running bitter on his tongue as he remembers the smell. Cliff's expectation, positioning himself in a taint-crushing straddle upon the window-sill's sharpness, was of the usual boyish reek, that familiar cheesy mix of dirty boxers, onion, plaque, and toe jam. What greeted him in the dark, however, was the smell of things forgotten and claimed by rot. Gagging, Cliff felt along the wall for a light switch, stubbing a toe on a rusty-nutted dumbbell set and knocking the wire loose from his denture's implant-anchors after tripping over an empty dog kennel. Once the switch was found and the room it served to illuminate revealed, Cliff bit his teeth back into place and squared himself to set to work.

The room was an absolute disaster. Fly strips hung

from the ceiling like bunches of grapes while still living juicy-bodied bluebottles buzzed in a cloud over a mountain of dishes in the kitchenette's sink. Source of the smell no doubt. Clothes were piled atop a bare memory-foam mattress on the floor. Cliff bravely produced a garbage bag from beneath the sink, holding his breath while in proximity to the dish pile, and shoveled in all the clothes he could fit. Hucked it out the window. Hands and knees and rolled the memory-foam mattress tight enough to shove through into the night. The television and game console was an inspired touch. Caught up in the intoxication of heroic banditry.

Cliff kicks the truck's ignition and backs out of the restaurant parking lot.

&

He's sat on the grass painlessly grinning in a candy-flipped trance, futzing with his new scar, watching the flames climb the sky in sync with the infernal build from the bottom of pummeling dubstep.

Abounding around him: Dancing shadows. Upraised arms and howling voices. Glittery sweat. All a bacchanal to laude the night.

The DJ's dedicants dragged the ruined couch from

the front lawn where Cliff had discarded it the night he made the house a home for Rory, and placed it sacrificially before the altar of PA speakers, turntables, and mixer-board on a foldout table. Set it on fire as the first track in the mix revved up. The foam beneath the cushions' faux leather balled to pucks of char, portending of the flame's future burning out. A bonfire's got to burn until the last bass drops the night into morning, so the early ravers dispersed into the woods that made up most of the property. They returned hauling all manner of kindling and fuel. Two tassel-titted girls brought forth a mossen log like a coffin. A tall form in a glow-in-the-dark G-string and rubber wolf mask re-wrestled itself from the thicket bearing a great spool of briary vines. Twigs and branches and shaggy fallen trees, rolled by the kicks of platform shoes and knee-high lace, combat boots and the liberated soles of naked feet. And the fire grew, as did the sound, as did the crowd.

Darkness fell full around the flames. Someone came with a lighting rig. Strobes and beams to cut bodies out of the smoke. A pickup truck, bed full of ice, dropped its gate, and revealed a clutch of dent-glitzed kegs. The sights and sounds, the voices and noises of humanity strung out raw and free, brought the clod-shouldered vagrants from the forest.

Rory'd say he'd not meant for it all to get so out of hand. On the inside he'd cleaned up enough for boredom to reinsert itself as the thorn in his side. Nothing stimulated him to rise from the mattress on the living room floor, but every piece of him cried out for something to move him. The 3D models of soldiers and aliens, zombies and gods, on the television screen that had served their tenure as distraction from the pains of withdrawal and convalescence now seemed to him flat and false avatars for empty worlds.

The phone rang this afternoon as he searched one of the game's battle maps for exploitable glitches. Usually Rory'd let it go to voicemail, add it to the garbled mass of hollow well-wishes and miss-yous, but today was the day for something new, for a change, for a return.

"Hello?" he'd said not bothering to check the caller ID. At this point he might've even taken up a robo-call's offer of extending the warranty on a car he doesn't have, if only for the sake of—

"Rory! Holy shit you're alive!"

"Yessir, indeed." Still not a clue who's on the other end of the line. Didn't matter.

"Fuck me, man! Where you at? You know

someone like broke into your house and shit? Dude no one's seen you in fuck who knows how long—"

"Yeah, yeah, I've been taking it easy for a bit. Got this place out near Grouseland State—"

"Yo! You got a cabin?"

"No, not exactly. Kinda, sure, yeah. Me and a buddy are like—"

"That's lit, so fucking lit. Where at? Who're you with? Fuck man! Nature and shit, I bet that's nice as fuck for real."

"Yeah, it's cool. You should come out some—"

"Done, dude. See you soon." And the line clicked out.

Rory laid back down and his phone dinged a text receipt: **Hit me with the address**

&

A month, gone:

"Rory?"

Cliff steps from the hall into the living room. The mattress is empty. The television leans against the wall, a crack webbing across its now forever dark face. It's noonish. It's hot. There's still broken glass on the floor, so Cliff wears his boots inside.

"Rory?"

Takes a cigarette from his chef's pants pocket. Lights it. Ashes on the floor. There's a half a bottle of some ominously cheap vodka on the counter.

"Rory? The fuck are you?"

Slept in his teeth last night, so his mouth is sore just like the rest of his head. Every syllable a pinch at his swollen gums and firecracker in his skull. Takes a pull from the warm bottle.

They'd had a few people over last night. They'd had a few people over every night since the party a week back. Mostly Rory's people. Cliff likes Rory's people. They're young and unbothered. Candles freshly lit.

"The fuck are you, Rory?"

The smoke had spread far off the property by the time Cliff had gotten closer to home, taken through the trees by the wind, setting a haze about the roadway. Smelled it before he saw it: oleaginous, plastic soot of a trash fire. Then the smoke gradually greyed the dark, a silent film's unrestored footage fading out before the final logo, and a bumper suddened from the screen. Cliff slammed on the brake.

"Goddamn!" Rolled the steering wheel to cross the doubled solid yellow. "Who the fuck, I mean who in God's greenest parks on the shoulder like that, on

58

a blind fucking turn! Goddamn idiots!" Laid on the horn to send the curse nowherewise.

The smoke thickened as he passed the cattywampus sedan. Lowered his lights, leaned over the wheel, squinted. Tongue fiddling with the wires in his head.

"Motherfucker."

There were more cars in front of the sedan, all nearly rolling off into the drainage ditch, lining the outside edge of the blind curve that opens to the final straightaway to Cliff's house.

Cliff cut the volume on the radio, easier to see when things aren't so loud. When the music fell, a firmer fundament rose untzing from where there should have been silence.

"Rory." Under his breath.

Menthol mingles with mouth-breather gunk, acetonic vodka, and brassy gum blood as Cliff perches his cigarette twixt his lips. Puts an arm through one shirt sleeve, then the next. Doesn't bother to button. Returns to the kitchen to grab the bottle by its neck. Steps out into the day through the back door.

It's just past noonish now. Hotter than all hell. Humid. The grass is still wet, the yard leading to the woods' eruption still trampled mud and ash. Ruined by foot and flame and that final deluging barrage from the fire engine's hose. Came rounding the far side of the house, tearing over the grass, siren blaring and lights flashing. Without so much as a warning, drenched it all. Knocked Cliff's legs out from under him, wind from his chest, replaced his teeth with a mouthful of mud and cigarette butts as the rave ran riot.

Looks over it all now after another swig against his hangover. Absolutely destroyed. Big black spot in the center of the yard like a bomb'd gone off. Once it dries it'll run back to the lifeless loam it had been when he'd moved out here three-and-some-such years ago. Planted the grass himself, first thing he did before even tearing the wallpaper down. Can't believe, chin trembling at it all, that he hadn't been the one to call the fire department or the cops or whatever, that he hadn't been the one to shut it all down. He'd let this happen, participated in it, *approved* it.

"I know, I know. It's ok, baby. But you've got to stop all this. You've got to stop all this." Her voice didn't even trip over the word *baby*, said like she always had, like she'd still loved him enough to tell him 'fuck off' to his face.

"She can't, like just uhm," Cliff sucked a wad of mucus come loose from tears brewing down his throat, "Just for a weekend. I mean, I've got the place all—"

"I'm sure you do, Cliff. But I don't know if Leah would—"

"No! She'd love it! We'd go hiking and fishing and, my property it, the whole thing's surrounded by woods and about a quarter mile or so into them, butts up on Lake Mikal, and I can get work off easy if we can plan ahead to—"

"Cliff."

"Yeah, sorry, uhm," could feel the hammer lifting to nail down the 'No.'

"Look, Cliff, I don't even know if she'd recognize you. I'm not sending my daughter to stay with someone who's a complete stranger to her."

He'd wanted to scream then. He'd wanted to find some way to reach through the phone and get his hands around her neck. He'd wanted to shout, 'I'm her fucking father! I'm fucking her father! I know I fucked up, but I've gotten everything together! You should see what I've done, what I've built out here! You think I did this shit for me? You think I'd have ever done all this fucking shit for anyone but her! My daughter? No! This isn't my house, this is her house! I did this for her!' So, Cliff wandered through the crowd and smoke, marveled a bit at the fire, and found the pickup truck with the kegs. Been coughing up black and green shit every morning since.

Hawks it into the mud beneath him. Takes another pull. Steps toward the forest.

"Rory?"

Water has gathered and stagnated in pools where the woodland begins its descent toward Lake Mikal. A film over the puddles. Swarms of gnats hovering. Late spring by now, so there's probably an oozy brood of black tadpoles flitting in clumps among the mud, twigs, and leaves unaware that they'll dry to raisiny compost within a few days. All this life at the edge of the forest. New fungi fanfaring from stumps that had dried to forget they were supposed to rot. Vines venturing a bloom or two more, another strangle further up their tree. All this life at the edge of the forest, excited and new and situated at the top of a slope that drains the water away, takes everything the firehose gave when it blasted the blaze down, hammering partiers to the ground, frying the DJs equipment to spark, sputter, and die.

There were arrests made. Intoxication charges. Possession. DUI. Pigs lined up just picking people off as they left wet and dripping, hoping to sleep the whole next day away. Cliff got a fine and warning against the future.

&

He's sat on the pebble and clay shore, painlessly grinning at the rise brought on by the spliff of the dirty fella next to him, when Cliff appears before the lake. Cigarette dangling, belly hung out sweating, looking like all greasy hell.

"Hey there, Cliff." Rory waves.

"I was calling for you." Cliff steps onto a rock, takes a swig. Looks down to keep his balance beneath him.

"I heard. I was here."

"Figured." Cliff looks up and notices one of the more intrepid of the county's unhoused population sitting next to Rory, picking hunks from the yellow callus that soles his foot. "Who the fuh, who's this, Rory?"

Rory looks over his shoulder like he'd forgotten the man was there and hadn't just been lecturing on the geological history, the *'deep time'* he'd called it, of the region. "Oh! I didn't, I guess I didn't catch your name. What was—"

"Jeremiah." The man said and brought a translucent, chalky chunk of dead skin to his nose. Sniffed and flicked it into the lazy lap of the lake on the shore. "Jeremiah Mikal."

Rory looks back at Cliff, eyes watering at the dryness of his mouth, "Jeremiah. Says his daddy dug the lake."

4

Laity and Dedicants

Posted twelve hours ago. One o'clock in the morning and even Brynn was there. A series of fifteen-second videos, shot with their new phone's camera. Blurs and strobes, bit-crushed screams and dumb-thudding bass.

Sasha rapidly thumbs the left side of her phone's screen, bringing her back to the first story Taylor'd posted in the last twenty-four hours: green grass abutting a paisley summer-shawl splayed blanketing and Sasha's flip-flopped foot twitching as she uttered something inane and torn by the wind; Taylor's xylophonic cackle, and a muffled bump to black as prelude to the next post; a still flyer for last night's Industry Blowout at the Bottom. Thumbs back once

65

more again to watch her foot twitch in her love's electronic eye.

A groan from the world: "Morning, Sash."

Eyes rise to Brynn, standing bottomless in an oversized t-shirt, fiddling a clementine between her fingers.

"Mind if I sit?"

"Yeah, uhm, go for it." Sasha presses the home button, exiting out of Instagram and back to the menu screen cluttered with icons, portals, ways-out-and-away-from—

"Studying?"

"What?"

Brynn nods toward the stack of textbooks, pages stuffed with notepaper, edges curling and frayed, blooming lichenly, pushed to the edge of the table where the nook longs to the window.

"Yeah, yeah, trying I guess." Sasha sets her phone screen-down on the tabletop as Brynn pulls the bench away and slides in.

Once sat, Brynn looks down at the clementine, turning it to find nub or navel, somewhere to insist her thumb through. Her hair is wet from the long shower she's just taken, dripping onto her shoulders and down her back, translucing the shirt against her skin. Her hands are shaking. The clementine slips from her grasp.

Sasha catches it rolling. Feels and finds a portion where the pith inside has come away from the flesh, a hollow pocket beneath the rind. Pinches it between her manicured thumb and forefinger. Tears a hole. Passes it back to Brynn, perched on a pedestal of acrylic.

"Thanks, Sash."

"Yeah, no problem." Catches full view of Brynn's face: puffy and red in the cheeks, neither ruddy or rouged, blotchy, the rash beginnings of stress acne flowering out from the bridge of her nose. Lips chapped shaggy. A hickey on her clavicle. Sasha looks away. Draws her phone back before her. Screen still shining, asks uninflected: "How was your night?"

"Oh my god..." Brynn drops the clementine again and puts her head in her hands. "Could you hear us?"

"What? No, I was—"

"My god, it's so embarrassing."

"No, I was just wondering because I—" Flips through the menu to find the Insta icon. Thumbs it.

"Ugh, why me, though, you know?" Clementine reretrieved. Rind rending away in hunks. "I mean, it's kind of my fault sure I guess or whatever, but like, ugh... a fucking dishwasher..."

"No, I was just wondering because… *shit*," The timeline has updated since Sasha'd set the phone down, burying Taylor's story in a queue of everyone else, to the back of the feed for having already been seen. "Here, give me like one second to find it again, I was only—"

"Just feels so gross, you know? Like, he was so just, like greasy or I don't know… I mean he's a nice enough guy and not super bad looking or anything just, like, a dishwasher at that awful fucking place and—"

"I was only asking because, uhm, because Taylor didn't come home, *come over*, didn't come over last night. But I saw that you were—"

"God, I feel like shit. And I can still taste him… Like not like his, you know what I mean, like the way he kissed and his tongue. God, he smokes so many cigarettes and sweats like the worst I've ever seen and smells like fucking onion or—"

"Found it!" Sasha's had to remember which of Taylor's several, and increasingly niche, accounts it'd been posted from. In this case it came under the authorship of their newest meme page, @InpatientRuth, which was more and more replacing the main account that they'd crafted together at a lunchroom table tail-end of high school's senior year. She thumbs through the resurrected stories to find again the—

"I mean, don't get me wrong, he's the nicest boy. A total sweetheart. A real peach, my dad might say, but he's—"

"See look." And Sasha turns the phone away from her face, shoves it up under Brynn's shame-glittered eyes: Still flyer in a field of rosy tangerine, after a progress bar ticks out its brief allotment, flips and gives again once more to the series of clips Sasha's watched the repetition of over upon over since she first sat to distract herself from study, tackily gumshoed into speculations about the happenings of a night she'd denied herself. From the speakers comes again the garble-fried music that's by this point taken full compositional form in her mind. In Brynn's eyes she can make out the shrunk, warped, and inverted image. Memorized thoroughly enough to time out perfectly, "See!" and ply her finger to the screen to stop the playback at a moment where the haze is clearest, where at the very least a strobe has illuminated the dancefloor enough to make out the separations between the bodies amassed in the dinge. Taylor's painted face in the selfie-shot foreground, "See! That's you right? Top left-ish, way in the back with—"

Brynn leans in and squints. "Oh my fucking gaw-aw-awh-duh…" hands back to her face. The palmed darkness provides a pitch canvas for yet another forgotten portion of the night to redraw itself. Clear enough on the screen: Will's hand down her pants, squeezing her ass beneath the denim, all in broad public. Work-shirt untucked and now she remembers how he'd pulled panty's lace aside and knuckled his way into, "Jesus fucking Christ, can you, just, not. Get that shit out of my—"

"No, no, it's whatever, babe. No shame. Get what you gotta get when you gotta get it."

Brynn thumbs a slice of the clementine into her cheek, crinkle of her brow indicating that her stomach would rather her mouth be empty. "I knew you'd shay that," through the juice.

"I was just wondering if you like saw Taylor at all while you were there or if—"

"I can't remember if I saw *anything* last night, Sash…"

"Yeah, alright," fronts the phone to herself again. Image still held on Taylor's painted face. Purple and neon orange glowing in the blacklight. Tongue out and shimmering in a grinful of shining teeth. "I was just wondering…"

"Plus, I mean. How is anyone supposed to

recognize anyone at that shit? Nobody is anything like they are in real life when they're at shows like that..."

&

They wake in a pile. All of them. Strewn and gathered. Asunder and sweating out of their sleep. All a mass breaking back to pieces, unable to reconstitute the heaving form they'd forgotten their fall from.

Taylor presses palm to crown and wipes a glitter-gritted curl of forelock from their brow. Eyes hot with salt and restless sleep. Runs a hand down their neck. Everything softer, apple swallowed more and more by everything getting softer. Cups thumb and forefinger an inch beneath each bared nipple to measure the months' recently collected heft. Smiles at the tender ache in the flesh. Everything getting softer. Sitting up against the faux leather of the couch front, legs stretching as much as the pile will allow. Unsticking ass cheeks from the tile floor, Taylor looks over the bodies still sleeping and smiles all the more.

The early afternoon sun invades through the window. Its light brings them all just to stirring. All as naked as themselves. A sea of skin here in this apartment, undulating in dreams. They're tied in among each and every other—limbs caught hooked and legged around, groins perched upon cocked thigh, hands full of cheek, breast, belly, ball, or cradling a trust-swept face against a chest's hearty regularity. It smells like low tide.

Breathes deep and a hand falls from up on the couch, catches their clavicle and blindly spiders to their chin. Taylor grabs and thumbs the hand's palm, spreading the sleepy fingers out, kisses each digit before setting it back to the side of its body. Rises from the floor. Turns to see who took the couch this time: two lithe, twinklingly shaven boys, entwined enough to be convincingly of one skin.

With their rise, Taylor's morning wood falls and the fullness of their bladder presses angry and hot. The path to the bathroom is automatic but hopscotching through cross-tossed limbs has Taylor pinching the tip of their penis against the shaken furiosity of their body's will to purge.

At the door the body nearly gets its way as some resisting force holds panel against frame. But the knob turns, and with one last hip-and-shouldered try again Taylor is able to push past the whateveristhere and into the bathroom. Inside is another form: long, lank, and glitter-crusted; still sporting the flop of a snarl-snouted rubber wolf mask. The form's foot, kicked out from the toilet atop which the rest of it slept, had been blocking the door. Now that it's been swept away, jabbed off the jamb by Taylor's need to piss, its body begins to stir.

"Luca, Luca," Taylor says, one hand mushing glans in palm and the other slapping the emaciated canine's hard, hairless flank, "Wakey, wakey, Luca. Get up. I gotta rock a piss."

Luca bolts up with a snarl and some weak nasally sound that's become what all recognize as his growl.

"Off, baby. Off the toilet, Luca."

It's all elbows, knees, and vertebrae as Luca clatters from the bowl and skitters over to the corner.

"Thanks hon."

Taylor's bladder purges. Apple juice yellow, hot and acrid, bubbling in the bowl with a vengeance, burning its way out, a micro-sharded silt stream. Explains the hollow feeling they've had since standing; scooped of innards and stuffed like a teddy with soft void, dizzy and floating, stitched back together along jagged seams, and aching so bad it almost feels good, affirmative that life hasn't yet left them in the dark. Torrent rolls over to tinkling and, shaking the rest to dribble, Taylor feels something tickle around their calf.

"Jesus Christ," and they almost kick Luca right in

his neon hammocked gnards, "Watch it! That's not for you! Get, get!" Ankle on rib.

A yip.

An apology.

"Alright, alright. C'mon. You're filthy." And Taylor pulls back the shower curtain, cuts on the faucet, lifts the plunger to send it all up and back down through the showerhead. "Let's get you cleaned up. C'mon. In, in." Pats his bony haunches as Luca shakily lifts a leg over the side of the tub. "C'mon, Luca, c'mon. I know you don't like it but c'mon. Such a dirty boy you are."

Already whimpering with his whole chest, heaving bellowfuls, tummy tightening and shaking his entire self, Luca paws with his knuckles at the basin's curve. Kicks back splash with gripless heels. The shower pelts his haunches, replacing the gunky smears of glitter and glue with patter-reddened flesh. Tries to scurry out and gets caught knotted-up sideways. Yelps.

"Luca! C'mon, baby, you've got to stand up now, gonna have to get on up so I get in and help." Taylor puts a leg into the lukewarm downpour, pats Luca's cowering shoulder, "C'mon, hon, up and up, let's go. Enough."

With Taylor now fully in the shower, blocking

74

most of the flow, Luca stands up to his full height. He's a big man, easily clearing a foot over Taylor. Looking down now, rubber mask dripping from its frozen grotesquery, horror film's villain in a thunderstorm, all drop-shouldered and pathetic, Luca raises big knucklesome hands from his side.

"No, no, turn around, no cuddles, let's get you washed clean."

Luca turns his back to Taylor. They pluck the bar of soap from the rack where it whitely molders and run it briefly in the water.

Hands lathered and slick, "Alright, take your nunnies off." Snaps the waistband against the plain of his lower back.

Luca yowls and starts in on another nasally growl.

"Don't get an attitude with me. Didn't wanna wash, shouldn't have slept in the bathroom. Should have slept in the yard like any other dirty dog. Time to be a people, Luca. It's morning enough now."

Pitiful whimpering as Taylor slips their thumbs through and pulls the skimp of fabric down off his waist and over his hips, exposing not much more than was already plain to see. Taylor flicks the wet wad out of the tub and onto the floor. Suds and rubs. Starts with Luca's tiny turned-over soup-cup glutes and follows the vertebrae right on up to his broad pustule-pocked shoulders. Big castile circles scented of lavender and patchouli unsticking it all from his skin, taken away in rivers and pooling between them. Water rises around their ankles as the flotsam, hair, and pigment gives the drain more than its perforations can handle. Reminds Taylor of the paint they'd forgotten is still caking their face and chest.

"Alright, baby, back to me now."

Luca turns around and again begins to lift his hands.

"Nuh-uh, hon, hands to ourself." Replenishes the lather on their palms and passes the slippery bar over to Luca, "C'mon, wash your business."

Cups his hands around the bar of soap, rolling it around in the bowl of his fingers. Fills it with water and releases the seal between his pinkies, draining the small deluge and filling the bathtub with the hollow sound of splash in rising water.

"Luca, don't play with it. Wash your business." Taylor grabs the bar back and rubs it into his palms themselves. "C'mon, enough. Gotta be a people for a bit." Rubs his great hands together for him, bubbles taking over as a hornet's nest does a stump. Guides his wrists down out of frame to where the tumescent whole of him hangs. "Wash it." Taylor says without looking down. Seen it plenty of times, whether bared or barely gathered in his G-string. Impressive hardware, terrifying.

Taylor turns toward the shower and lathers their face. At the behest of finger and faucet, paint comes away in clots and flakes. Can feel it lifting from their skin, the mask they'd worn all night, some stripe-faced abomination of abandon. Water runs over their clearing skin as popping lather builds. All rhythm, all music, the circles rubbed around their ears, cheeks, chin, forehead; the frazzling on Taylor's closed eyelids, the steady and heavier dribble into the building slosh-pond at their feet. Now rising: an accelerating *fut-fut-fut.*

Taylor spins out of the water at a weight on the back of their neck. Luca, hog in hand, hard-up and blooming bubbles at the bell-end. Wet hefted sighs from within the wolf.

"Jesus Christ, Luca." Swats his hand off and away from the veiny worth, "Could you fucking not!"

Luca recoils to the wall and falls into the tub's foot-founded tide.

"Enough, enough. C'mon, c'mon. Gotta be a people now." And Taylor bends down to get a furl of the rubber wolf-mask in their hands. "Enough, gotta be a people now. Gotta behave like a people, Luca. You've got work today, remember?"

The mask comes off with a deep sucking sound, revealing Luca's tomato red, heat-rashed face, seething with shotgun-blast cystic acne. Tosses the mask out of the shower to join the G-string. Husky-sapphire eye, bloodshot and full of embarrassed tears. Luca hyperventilates through his nose, jets of clear phlegm flying forth and retreating into the cavern, as Taylor bends back down to unlatch the buckle of the spittle-shimmered ball-gag that's propped Luca's mouth open all through last night and this morning. Luca's face collapses into a teeth-grinding sob, hissing between incisors.

"Really shouldn't wear this thing while you sleep, hon," Taylor says, holding it dangling in front of their face. "You know, it's just not—"

Luca: wide-eyed, baring his teeth. Stomach tight and ribs pressing ridges through the skin.

"Hey, it's alright, hon. It's—"

Luca lunges, blasting up with a splash, and wraps his arms around Taylor's waist. Hangs his whole weight off their hips and buries his face in the soft emptiness of their belly.

Taylor places a hand atop Luca's head, where the curls thin and give way to hot skin. Luca's shoulders shake. "It's alright hon, it's ok, just—"

And Luca's mouth relaxes where Taylor's fine

blondery blooms at the base of their creamily soft penis and purse-tight scrotum. A kiss there, then the tongue. A groan from deep in Luca's chest as his mouth open's gag-wide to slurp up the whole of Taylor's tackle.

Reaching down and pinching his nose hard before he can start in animal again: "Nuh-uh, no. Not today, not today…"

Outside the bathroom, in the kitchen, the others are gathering to assemble a breakfast: sourdough toast, orange juice, stove-top espresso with oat milk, and a cast iron skillet sizzling a pile of veggie hash, scrambled up with that vegan cheese that doesn't melt so much as it laminates.

&

From the table nearest Sasha's at Caffe Destare, a woman on the phone: "…No, see that's the whole issue… uh-huh, no I know, but… Look, Travis's convinced himself he's an Aquarius… Yeah, no but… I know none of… No, Mom, listen, you live your whole life thinking you're one thing and… Yeah, Mom, no I get it, I know none of…"

Sasha's been sat listening to this half-conversation for over ten minutes now.

Twenty-five minutes ago, Taylor'd texted: **Hey, hey, babe. Headed to Ds if you're up yet be there in fifteen or so probably. Good morning :)**

Sasha'd replied immediately: **Goodmorning hon I will see you soon love you!!!**

Years and the thought of meeting up with Taylor still makes Sasha quiver and break out sweating. Her belly doesn't fill with butterflies, but moths—big, feathery-winged, clumsy moths bumbling around a too-small hollow, slamming themselves blind and lame against the pulsing warmth of her heart's light. But, listening minute upon minute to the astrological inanity cutting through the coffee shop's too-loud music, the warm swarm inside her has started to turn, every flap and flutter breaks a wing and loses a landing leg. Soon it will all be so many rattling husks piled in her guts.

Sasha looks down at her phone, finds again Taylor's stories and checks to see if there's any new posts.

"Yeah, yeah... for sure... Uh-huh... Ok, but here's what I'm saying Mom, because they're two very different... Uh-huh, no, no... No, it's not just about that like, it's just that he won't, Travis won't admit to it. He won't like *be* what he *is* with anything... yeah, yeah... but it's just... yeah... but it's just that he's *not* those things he wants to be..."

From behind the counter, the barista, as the bell announces an entrance: "LATE! LATE! LATE, DUDE! LATE!"

Two silhouettes cut out of the doorway by the shattering afternoon sun. One taller than the entrance bends itself in half to enter the shop. Once inside, it steps to the register, head hung around its chest, massive tarantula hands held out in a gesture of supplication. Festering face lit at the register. Wet lips mouth words of apology.

The barista: "Yeah, whatever Luc. Just get your apron on and get back here, I can't, I've got shit to do…"

Still in the doorway is another shape. Smaller, softer, cotton-blonde forelock hallowing as a halo.

Sasha's stomach plummets. Hands numb up to her elbows. Lifts an arm to wave but Taylor catches her eye before her wrist can engage.

They float when they walk, frictionless with the world around them, just as likely to pass through obstacles as to have them briefly animate to move from their path. As Taylor glides, Sasha finds herself rising.

"I just don't know if I can keep being with someone who… Yeah, no I remember, he didn't believe in the moon landing, right… but this is,

Mom… Yeah, I know I know how to pick 'em, never let me live a single one down… but this, yeah, no, this is different… this is like saying you don't believe that the moon is there at all in the first place, or that it's just a hole in the sky…"

They embrace with the small table still between them, pressing its edge eachly into their thighs. Soft are their lips against their lips. Tender is it all. Immutable the smiles as their lips part.

"But what am I supposed to tell him? He's *actually* being a total fucking Capricorn by refusing to believe that the—"

"You didn't get anything?" Taylor asks, indicating to the emptiness of Sasha's table.

"Oh, no, not yet, I was waiting for you to see if—"

"Everyone wants to be an Aquarius, especially if they're on either side of the cusp like… Yeah, no I know I'm being a total, yeah… but, it's just, you are what you are! Right, Mom? Right… Yeah, but try telling that to a Pisces, much less a Capricorn… I mean have you ever not wanted—"

"My treat then!"

"No, no, babe, let me get it, let me get it." Sasha turns to dig in her purse. Clasp in hand she rounds, but Taylor is already at the register waiting perfectly postured. Sasha sinks back to her seat.

"*All. The. Time.* Right? But I'm a Virgo. Who wants to be a Virgo... I know, but that's what I'm trying to say is that—"

Taylor leans on the counter to sort through a wad of cash from their fanny-pack. Mouth moving in pleasant conversation with Luca at the espresso machine. His sad, heavy eyes glisten as he nods and listens. Smiles at a joke. Taylor gestures with a small, soft hand, making some point that only a granite pillar could be heartless enough to disagree with.

"—you don't get to choose that stuff, the whole universe has... no, no, no, not conspired, Mom, none of it's ever done *against* you, which is what I'm trying to explain, the universe isn't like trying to say—"

Even the 'thank you' is invigorating. Lips and teeth and tongue all coming together in an earnest moment of gratitude, earnest to the very bottom. No one ever thanks anyone like that for anything.

"—you don't get the option, the box is... yeah, you said box, I didn't say box, but the... fine, place, sure, that's better... location even... I mean, wherever, wherever the universe puts you, that's where you are and you can't just decide that you're supposed to actually be an Aquarius when the whole everything has decided that you indeed are in fact—"

Again, Taylor approaches the table and Sasha rises

to receive them. Another kiss. Coffees down. Sasha sits and looks up as Taylor cocks their neck curious, looking up and off toward the speaker nestled in the ceiling's corner.

"What is it?" Sasha asks.

Taylor blinks and looks down to her, "Oh nothing, just love this song."

5

Balneary

Rose with the rest as dawn's pinking paled through the gaps in the trees. Haze briefly perfumed with a glow, now turning with the crash of heavy day, pouring the suffocating soup of a summer arriving once again too soon.

"Jer'miah, comin' today or…?"

Jeremiah looks down at his duff-dusted pallet before he answers the voice a tree or two away. A winter coat stiff and thin as cardboard with a decade's sweat and mud. Sog-soft cowboy boots, weathered to withers, bunch together well-enough to act as a pillow. Got a real duvet for a top-sheet, rescued weeks ago from an apartment complex's dumpster.

Jeremiah grumbles. Voice growls like a 72oz

Styrofoam cup, full half-up with quarters and shaken. "I don't reckon, no… Uhm, not today. I've got to," and he motions toward his sleeping pile, "got to clean up, maybe."

"Alright, well, you wan' us a'bring you back something or anything?"

Jeremiah's already turned away from the source of the voice. Looks out into the forest. Catch the last moments of morning's glorious blush. Smell the soil waking up. Blooms of honeysuckle kicked off their feet by the rank nastiness of dogwood. Sweet rot from below. All of it, though, all of it kept tight and quiet and low by the morning's final breeze off the lake, the last sigh of night, cool and calm and just good enough to have Jeremiah forgetting for a breath that today marks three days since he's last eaten.

"Jer'miah, you listening? Want us a'bring you back something from down in town or anything? We all got to get to stepping afore it gets hot as it's gonna be—"

"I'll be fine." Stomach kicks like a squirrel de-hibernating.

"Alright then, brother. Alright."

So, they get to stepping. Dragging their ragged feet through the loam and leaf, following the rough path they've stomped over the past week-and-change. Never stay in one part of the woods long enough for the environment to grow up around them, take their structure into consideration. Leave it all leveled in their wake, freshly flattened for new growth. Too much risk in staying put.

Common knowledge among the townsfolk that Jeremiah and his vagrant ilk have been camping out in these woods, in the offseason on the Grouseland tract itself, for years and years and years. Closed down the shelters a decade-and-a-half or so back, and if city police catch a fella sleeping on the sidewalk they're just as likely to arrest him as they are to drive him out to the middle of nowhere and kick him to the shoulder. So, the unhoused brought themselves nowhereward on their own, and have taken quite a liking to it. Everyday they rise with the sun, their instinctive diurnality uncorrupted by the slant rhythms of university-town life. Once risen they descend to the bustle.

Some in Jeremiah's little cluster have jobs landscaping or in construction. Some are in recovery—most though are on their way back into the throes that first threw them—and must get to town early enough to get in line to stave off the terminal pitch. All of them, even the employed, do hours of panhandling each day. All to say, as their footsteps fade away, that Jeremiah garners no pleasure from having kept them waiting for him with his silence and grumbling. Can't bear the thought of it all—the town, the people, food and water—not on a morning as delicate as this.

Sooner or later it's all going to crash. Even those who've forsaken themselves of the world, uncogged from the grand grist mill, will be caught and killed in the grinding halt of the machine's terminal failure.

&

Steam fog's fallen by the time Jeremiah gathers gumption enough to trek the twenty yards of bosk between his pallet and the lake. No longer are lacy, carnation-colored nymphs floating over the face of his father's final lasting achievement. The surface of Lake Mikal is black and motionless on this windless morning. At its edges, where Jeremiah's horn-crusted feet soak submerged over a bed of algae-slick pebbles—bought as refuse from the granite quarry two counties south, brought to line the shore here, keep down all that had been drowned—, the Lake's wrinkling winks streaks of white sunlight razoring into Jeremiah's eyes, rendering him progressively blind to his wavering reflection's face.

Looking up and away from the shimmer, Jeremiah searches the pockets of his grimy fishing vest—the trusty garment he's not been without since he first fell from the commonest graces of hearth and home—for the hard-resined roach he remembers hiding away before draining the dregs of his 40oz and slipping to sleep.

As he digs, hopping clod-fisted pocket-to-pocket, his belly growls another drool-jowled beg.

Difficult to keep the body in check. Hardest part, keeping the fleshy ape away from the soul's controls. Nothing can be done about the greater world, that's held in much larger hands, but this sopping mess the heart's piloting has got to be kept in line. Starve it of everything now and again and again and again and—

Now: Found it. Rolls the roach between his thumb and forefinger, loosening the bud from the build-up. Enough bunched there in the paper for one teensy drag, enough to make a morning, enough to forget himself for the water. The lighter is easier to find, always in the same breast pocket.

Flame to paper.

Paper to lip.

Smoke to lungs.

In a puff the little bug is spent.

The small high rises and Jeremiah peels off his

clothes. Fishing vest comes away from shoulders to be folded flat over a rock tabling out of the shallows. Next the t-shirt: a threadbare thing a size too big for Jeremiah's fast-wilted frame, a souvenir from Grouseland State Park printed with the profile of a black-braided native and the slogan 'A Place For Peace.' Been clung to his skin since his last swim. Comes away with an audible tear. Off now, tossed atop the rock, atop the folded vest. Jeremiah's pallid flesh is greeted by a sun angrier than it ought to be. He welcomes its gold, free to fry as much as it desires. The camouflage cargo shorts fall next. Something paler, more the failure, hangs in still air.

First time he was naked, truly naked—not as at birth surrounded by machines clothing the air with their hums and beeps and buzzes, nor as at defloration crammed into the back seat of a father's sedan or behind a dumpster in an alley or quietly grunting in a basement, nor any of the other everydays when the body is freed but the world made stays solidly in play—, first time he was truthfully naked was seven years after he'd tipped his tin john-boat in the center of this slate-still lake to see if the bottom of it all was far down enough. Lissa-Mae, rest her soul if there is one, had stayed up all into the night with him, well-past the baggie's last little bits, coming down and talking everything to pieces around the dwindling embers of their campfire. She'd taken him the minute the last of the light went out, when the night around them was blued in full by the moon before the horizon cracked open again.

Silver-white slashes of sun now slice the whole of Jeremiah's reflected body, cutting him up as if to illustrate the miracle of corporeality in this obvious void. The water is kind around his ankles and, the tiny high hitting the heights of its rise, his ankles are kind in turn to the water. He takes a step deeper. A step deeper. A step deeper until the surface has risen to his belly, the weight of the lake pressing in where there is nothing at all to push back. Know from experience that this is where the ridge lies: Water up past his waist and the rest of the lake pits and falls away deep, deep to the memory of its flooded holler. Any further out and he'll have to swim. So, with a sink and lunge, Jeremiah dips his crackle-crusted beard into the water and pushes off the pebbly bottom, into the dark under the surface.

There was a moment right after the john-boat flipped, after a finger of the lake had made its way up a nostril, when he thought that maybe he should have *at least* called into work, let them know he wasn't going to make it in ever again—but the bottom couldn't be that far down. Daddy couldn't have managed to drown that much in reality.

Once the lake is full around him, once his hair is wet and his chest heaves a heft heavier, Jeremiah turns over on his back and floats. There's no current, save for what the lazy carp and catfish can stir—Papa never managed to put in the pump, never managed to plumb it toward the city to render it reservoir—so the slightest heel kicks will take him as far as he needs to go: The center, the opposite shore, back to his piled clothes, it should all be effortless from here. From above he is a tear in a sheet of black satin, steadily threading and threatening to sever the implacability in two. The water's in his ears, humming something deep and cetacean. It climbs capillarily through his beard to line his lips. It tastes vegetal, of algae and all those drowned trees; mineral, like sand or concrete.

The finer details of the operation were never conveyed to him. Remembering his father's face—the few times Jeremiah'd gotten a straight look at it in the twilight of his last Mayoral term—fallen with age and disgrace, sagging under the invisible weight of failing the people's faith (a sapphired joy, though, buried in the eyes, gleaming satisfaction of an aged man having gotten his way), Jeremiah doesn't imagine the finer details were something his father'd thought about very much once the plan was in place and the land out from under its ownership. A big feat to move all this water. "Time and effort's all anything's ever taken," his father'd say, "time and effort and you can move the whole world an inch, a mile, hell, put out the sun if you want to!" Time and effort trickled the water in, re-routed from a tributary somewhere north and nearer the state-line before it could kiss in with the runoff-thickened way of Domino Creek. Wet gave to rise and soon enough the valley's slopes were populated with gawkers watching over weeks as the glittering shoreline swallowed goat pastures, apple groves, storage sheds, and, soon enough, a white-sided farmhouse perched on a soft, shady promontory.

"Your daddy ain' done nothing." Lissa'd said after snorting the last clump. She looked up at the stars, sniffling back the drip, "Didn't make the lake, water did. Your daddy ain' done nothing."

"No, I mean he, uhm," whatever they were snorting, it wasn't blow. Shit burned different. The high didn't increase the frequency and volume of thoughts, but instead scrambled the signals, bleeding pixel and fuzz across frame and frazzling all the borders, every idea lost to the image of another, swallowed and digested to so much shit. "Uhm, he made the, he told them to, like—"

"Water did. Water did. Listen. No," and that's when she scooched and got up close to him, right to where he could smell her, smell the dirt, the cheesy grease of the unwashed, the history he'd yet to live. She put her hand on his thigh and said, "The water and like the land or whatever, they did it, they made the lake. Your daddy ain' done nothing because, I mean look, the water, the land I mean the land was always ready for flooding, always made for it because it could be filled in the first place because that's how it was made and that's what water does, goes where it'll stay, right? So all the land needed to be a lake was to have the water in it to fill enough to be, look, your daddy ain' done shit but—"

At the moment of breaking, boat flipping and sending down everything that filled it, the water became inevitable, there was panic, sure and honest panic. Even if it had been on purpose initially, even if Jeremiah could remember taking the day off to go fishing, to find the bottom, to at the very least never go back to work, the minute he hit his father's water the animal inside kicked his legs for him and had him splashing against whatever will toward stillness he'd had.

It's got to be quieted, that stubborn animal inside so bent on life. It's got to be quieted; though, not to make dying easier, but to clarify the distinction *between* living and dying, to draw the actual differences against each other. The animal, hungry and thirsty and totally without reason, sees all things other than now as death—if it looked from the other side of the void toward life, it would place its fear there in the light and call it darkness. This is not the way of things. And if it is, what more hope could there be than gilded nil?

So, Jeremiah fought against the splash and kick and even, in a moment of minor heroism, against the will to breathe. Emptying his lungs with a foamy blast, he sank.

Every breath now holds him afloat. Every exhale and his belly falls below the surface. Without the inhale, heart calm, Jeremiah knows where he'll go.

Down deaf below. The lake was still and green, no sounds save those made before dying. He wasn't dying, not yet then, though his lungs ached to be filled and his heart raced, searching the blood as it passed like an addict ransacks their sock drawer for a crumb of whatever they said they'd never need again. Not yet dying then, still a minute or two away. Sinking, the lake weighed heavier with every foot he fell. The water around him felt as stone, pebbling his joints. Lungs fire and heart a crumbling brick of salt, Jeremiah's eyes opened and beheld before him an endless forest.

And she tasted of earth, every moment of her. Tongue shot into his mouth like a lump of wet clay. Her callused hands, with their rows of tendons like piles left behind a plough, fingertips stained rusty with blood and nicotine, dug fierce into his shoulders. Jeremiah found himself on the ground, head hitting hardpack, Lissa burying him beneath her. Kisses and falling rocks. Slate dark teeth gnashing in the night. Cloth coming away in shreds. The quivering of his skin in the moonlight. She'd bit his lip at some point. His mouth filled with blood. It dripped from her lips as she rose from the kiss she'd foundered to find him inside of her. Blood in shimmers from her chin, down her neck, and breaking out in vascular creeks over the quake-wrought hardness of her body. Granite or marble or something older—a stone of stones, the conglomerates that build mountains, the myriad rates of wear and weather, cleavage and luster, crystal and grain, a multitude of unwavering stillnesses and tremor toward cinders. Felt like she was going to break something, a wrist or whole limb or the very center of him, as her pelvis ground and ground.

Stretches where neither of them were breathing. Aches building in their muscles. All softness petrifying.

Starts in the left ankle, little quartz worm of pain, before exploding out and up his calf. The left heel won't kick anymore, so the rest of the leg takes it. But the pain is there too, finds its way up to his hip and locks it in lactic cement. Jeremiah's belly backflips and a gasp catches cough as his abdomen heaves. A cupful of black water fills his throat. The gagging exhale, sput and bubble. Both legs locked now. And Jeremiah sinks. In the water his eyes open: the submerged forest and valley's slopes are nowhere to be seen. In the black, darkness of life drowned and steeped for decades, there is nothing to be seen. Nothing to be felt but the pang of an empty belly.

Life and death are the open spaces on either side of pain. Only one plane guarantees no return to agony.

&

But, the little animal inside is always inside:

Jeremiah wakes walking. How he'd managed to swim from the center, he does not know. Where in the woods he is, he does not know. He's got a briar branch stuck to the sole of his left foot, thorns sinking

97

deeper with every crunching step. His tummy woke him.

Got his bearings there in the submerged forest—for just a moment. Managed to calm his heart and get his head out front, body fished out behind him. Took a handful of the still water, scoop and pull. His lungs screamed. Heart rate slowed to a thundering adagio. A kick and scoop and pull.

Where his bleeding feet are taking him he cannot say—cannot say because he neither knows, nor can he speak. Tongue's hanging out of his mouth, dried up from panting.

The whole all around him was untouched in its green haze, fish poking out of algae fluffed branches of birch and oak and pine and who all could know what else. It was all still—his lungs screamed—there, as if it didn't know it had been drowned. Heart slowed to a stop. Scoop and pull and the black fell across his eyes. His lungs quieted.

The little animal inside widens its eyes, heart hopping, as the forest falls away for a clearing and the bare porch of a vinyl-sided house. The little animal sprints. The little animal ascends the porch stairs and slams into the sliding door. The little animal inside paws at the glass. The animal finds the handle.

Unlocked! The animal opens the door and slips inside.

The air smelled painfully clean. His chest gurgled, and he hacked against his life coming back in a bleachy gasp. Eyes hot, nose runny, something stiffening his left arm—a needle attached to all manner of dripping complexity. Taste of the lake still on his tongue.

There is a kitchen. A refrigerator. An empty refrigerator. Jeremiah's stomach howls as he slams the fridge door shut. Cabinets all empty as well. Nothing. Nothing in this house.

"How're we feeling, son?" Eyes rose to suspenders and a buttoned-down swell of belly. That whiskey-rouged face. A hand on his shoulder—commiserative and terrifying.

Hot around his ears and now the sound of a television somewhere. The animal turns and Jeremiah sees blue flickering on the wall around the corner.

"Heard tell you fought real hard, son. Gave my lake the what-for kicking your way to rescue." Hand squeezed and Jeremiah became aware of the rest of his body. The ache a searing thread woven through muscle and tendon and anchoring itself down in his bones and joints.

Fear now. Pain in his foot. The briar branch had

dislodged in the sprint, mud caked where there was blood, but the flesh still hates. And the animal is afraid, aware, awake.

Tears poured at the knowledge of his body, of its resilience, of its strength. The sobs against life and its guarantee of agony shook his frame, shook the hospital bed. Slosh of curd and clod from the bedpan beneath him.

Rounding the corner, peeking out beneath a granite countertop, Jeremiah finds a mattress on wood flooring, a hump shivering under the covers, illuminated by the television. The little animal finds a plate piled with uneaten food and a plastic bottle half-full up with something bright orange.

The animal sprints again. Crams handfuls of bready something into Jeremiah's mouth. Unscrews the lid of the bottle and chugs down its saccharine citrus contents. Looks the quivering, fester-faced form in the eye—only one since the other is swollen shut beneath a blood-spotted bandage.

The little animal inside growls, shakes the bottle, and asks: "Do you have another?"

Tears welling over blue diamonds. The pale, shaking lump on the mattress says nothing in reply, having heard in its hallucinatory stupor the words: "I'll eat your mother."

6

Misericord

'...that is, however, not to say that Aquarians are
petty. The reality is quite the contrary. The
enlightened Aquarian, aligned with their sign and
universal coordinates, remembers *without* holding
grudges. He or she harbors in their mind every
history and personality they come across in their
lifetime, connecting the dots between disparate
ideas and people, amassing their experience of
others into a continuously growing community.
Their place within this community, as cool
headwater over a stony riverbed, flowing to
slowly shape and soften all they contact, is a
sacred position to the enlightened Aquarian. This
is what makes Aquarians ideal partners for nearly

every sign and, conversely, what renders nearly
every sign unfit for partnership with
Aquarians..."

The screen blurs as Travis' eyes oscillate again out of focus. A crusty blink and the office comes back hazy, crystalizes into its dust and cobwebs. The soda-lines climbing the wall pop and hiss for the first time this morning. Travis looks to the desk's second monitor, quartered split-screen by security camera's view of dining floor, bar, kitchen window, and the alley where employees smoke their shifts away. Will's just walked in for the prep and lunch shift, looking as bedraggled and mendicant as ever. Filling a take-away cup with the foul off-brand energy drink they keep on line for frat-star Jaeger-bombs.

Means Travis's forgotten to sleep. Will coming in tells the time as near ten in the morning. Forgot to sleep, getting sucked into these astrology blogs. Been sat here like this—sweatpants bunched around his ankles and sneakers, belly hanging over his rub-rashed, too-small but never complained over penis—for six or so hours. Ass asleep, balls bruised from a late-night beating, eyes wide as he flicks between webpages examining the finer points of the Aquarian and Capricorn:

'Traditionally represented by the image of a half-goat-half-fish chimera, Capricorns find themselves in a difficult position. This dual form, made all the more challenging with the obstinate nature of the ram heading up the sign, renders the immature or naïve Capricorn a spiritual vagrant, a wanderer whose desire for 'creature comforts' is forever unfulfilled as there is no single environment to which they are suited. Therefore, the enlightened Capricorn, rectifying this fact with themselves, sets about *creating* their own environment, suited to their individual needs...'

Third morning in a row here like this. First Morning: returning from returning from work after Lissa'd bawled him out of the doorway, across the lawn, back into his sedan, launching first the copy of the *Daodejing* she'd been reading at his turned back as he locked the door, surprise bringing him to face her standing there at the end of the foyer hall and a shimmer of something zoomed by his head to shatter into a sudden effulgence of patchouli and sandalwood, scent giving rise to a whatingodsholyname and a brass singing-bowl zinged to shatter one of the door's window panes, fumble with his keys, and Travis managed to get the door back open before all manner of other fetish and spiritual tchotchke could rain down on him, he woke with the desktop's keyboard stuck to his face, held there by sticky sweat and the chubby cling of his baby-soft cheek. Keyboard coming away, leaving a ruby-sumped honeycomb on the left side of his head for most of the day, summoned back to the monitor a webpage he'd forgotten he'd opened:

UNDERSTANDING the AQUARIUS:
An Examination of the Enigmatic Water-Bearer
By Madam Q. von Luna Esq. PhD. MD. Star-Seed.

Beneath the title was an illustration, assumedly medieval in origin, of a pale, naked man, hairless and unhung, with an upturned urn against his hip, pouring feathery water into a green river. Near mindless with his flick of the mouse, he highlighted the picture, saved the .jpeg, and, after navigating the baroque decision-trees of this operating system's pulldown menus, set the image as screensaver and background so that when he awoke on the second morning of his exile, this time with a knot brutally numb in his neck, he could flash himself with the pixel-poor visage of his truth—

"But that's, that's just not," a year and some change ago, just moving in, months before the marriage, Lissa: "You said the 9th, right?"

"Yeah, January—"

"That's Capricorn." Dropped her dirty backpack on the kitchen table. Clang and scuttle of glass and metal. The bag sagged.

"Oh, I guess I've always just said I was an Aquarius." Travis crossed from his spot leaning on the sink and grabbed the bag by a sticky strap. Placed it on the tile floor. "Never really—"

"Wait? You just, oh my god!"

"What's the, are you alright?"

Lissa: hands to face, covering her eyes. Behind palms, her mouth opened and closed as if attempting to dislocate her jaw, tongue screwing around in the toothy cavern. Travis'd come to recognize this configuration as the prefatory phase of an inevitable fit. What the nature of the paroxysm stood to be, whether joyful hysterics or a collapse into flesh-rending howls and bleats, he had no reliable model for prediction. So, he did what he always did: Walked over to her and took her to his chest, cushioning against any potential explosion with the softness she claimed to love.

In the harsh light of his kitchen's midday, against all the laminate and white, the condition Lissa's life had put her in shined as dark stars in a dying sky. Pitted scars and fresher seepings, self-inflicted wounds from nervous scraping, nails dragged through the gullies set out on her arms by constantly tight tendons and sandstone musculature. The washed-out pale of her face beneath the years of dust and grime—all taken initially, when he'd met her at Rook's, October steadily novembrating around them, as sunkiss or rouge. Sat next to him, close, smiling. Plopped her bag, *clank*, on the rail running round the foot of the bar. Ordered a gun-coke, no ice, extra fruit.

'Most Aquarians in their youth (and sadly, many still into their adulthood) find themselves lonely in the crowds that spontaneously come to surround them. Due to their *spiritual radar apparatus*, a feature of the Aquarian mind shared only by Libras (and used by even the most enlightened Libras to narcissistic, egoizing ends—see my post from February titled: *The Hand That Holds the Scales*), Aquarians are attuned to take notice of

the ways in which others create connections, through shared interests, similar senses of humor, commonalities of worldview, analogous modalities of vocation or occupation, but they are not equipped with the necessary *materiality anchors* that serve to tether most other signs to the non-spiritual, corporeal elements of existence. Aquarian Flux, the property that renders them both fluid and vessel, makes it difficult for the young and naïve Aquarian to handle social engagements. It takes enlightenment for Aquarians to properly play the part expected of them by their societies and cultures while still maintaining the freedom of their soul. Otherwise, the Aquarian will live the whole of their earthly existence at a remove, unable to reach out and touch what they are being told is there everywhere by everyone...'

Her voice came louder as she turned to face him: "Well?"

He'd pickled himself for no particular reason, just something to forget what he wasn't doing. Staring at the slurried amber dregs collected at the bottom of his glass, contemplating the contemplation of another one-more-again pint, lost to the din. She jabbed him in the flub gathered about his belt-sinched waist and, shouting this time: "Well!"

"*Well what!?*" Jiggle of jowl as his head shot up from the pint glass. "What? Well what?" Growling.

Her grin, audible in her voice before, widened at his outburst and flowered into a tongue-bit giggle.

"What? What do you—"

"I was," stifling the laugh, "I was asking you if you wanted to buy me a drink."

"What?" Couldn't hear her. Hand over her mouth.

"I was—"

And he leaned in, pursuing her words with a cupped ear.

Her hand found his shoulder, drew him closer. Breath on his neck the heat and odor of moldering mulch. "I was asking if you wanted to buy me a drink."

'...thus, it is often that the naïve Capricorn finds themselves in relationships in which they are an object possessed.

Exoticism is the chief burden of the Capricorn, total uniqueness in a sea of ubiquity. Difference abounds in the Capricorn's world. In their eyes all is discrete, separate, surrounded by invisible but

impenetrable notional walls...'

"Jesus fucking Christ!" Comes up from his chest. The wood of the office door barks, knocked near off its hinges.

Eyes to the security monitor. Dining room empty, no bustle about the kitchen, concrete dearth in the alley, bar deserted save for in the corner of the screen: two wavering blobs, shadows cast from some presence right outside the—knocking comes again, harder.

"Just one, give me just one fucking," rockets up from the wheelie-chair. Clatters to the floor as he bends down to pull up his sweatpants. Crust of forgotten discharge crackles and flakes off his belly. Soreness pruning up in his lower back as his frightened balls climb for cloister.

Muffled from the other side of the door:

"See yeah, I told you he was probably—"

"I don't have time for this, all very irregular."

"—in there, just give him a—"

"Highly, highly irregular. You people are—"

"Mind if I, I've got shit to do in the kitchen, can you just—"

"Better to have a witness."

Again with the knocking.

Travis: "Just one goddamn second! Christ!" Knees offer a gunshot pop as Travis manages to coincide the height of his rise with grabbing the knob. "Now what in all Christ do you fucking—"

Two figures there in the door as the opening gives way to a wall of leathery cologne. The effulgent dressed in a blue two-piece and tie, briefcase dangling by his side, cheeks red up with impatience. Behind him: Will—scraggle-faced, stringy-headed, red-eyed with sleeplessness and too much working.

"See, told you he'd be—"

"Mr. Alcott?" The suited man asks, breath peppermint crisp even at this distance.

"Who's asking?" Travis crosses his arms and leans against the doorway.

"I'm a service representative on retainer for McClaw and Nesbitt Divorce Attorneys. On behalf of," produces a manilla envelope from beneath the flap of lapel barring his chest, "on behalf of Lisa, no," squints at the case details scrawled atop the envelope, "Lissa, *Lissa?* Yeah, Lissa-Mae Tristina? Jesus Christ, you people. On behalf of Lissa-Mae Tristina Alcott you, Travis Gertrude Alcott, have been served." Holds out the envelope for Travis to take.

And there it is. Just there and over and—

"Sir, you are Travis Gertrude Alcott, correct?"

110

"Uhm, yeah. Yes. I am."

"I need you to take these documents. I have another appointment before lunch and—"

"Wait can you just give me—" Looks up from the envelope to the redolent man's steely eyes. Nothing but everything being held back there on his face. Travis' own cheeks boiling in bloody contrast to this man's sheen. "Can you just give me one, uhm, just one second here and—" Chin bunching, shaking lip and cheek alike. Hot salt and blur.

"Please. Take these documents. I have another appointment before lunch. Don't make this any—"

"No, no, no, wait. Can we just, here let me, let me call her real quick and this is all so goddamn unnecessary just because I don't want to be a fucking, just because I don't feel like a—"

The Service Rep turns to Will. "Are you prepared to confirm under oath that you witnessed me serve these documents to Mr. Alcott?"

Will: "I, I guess, no wait. Your middle name is—?"

"Are. You. Prepared. To. Confirm. Under. Oath—"

"Yeah! Alright, fucking creep."

"Good enough for me." Drops the envelope onto the floor. Heel turns and disappears.

There is a moment. Just there and over.

Travis is looking down. Envelope fuzzed out by

tears. Only a different color than the colors around it. Just there and over.

"Hey man, uhm… I think we're, shit. We're out of tater tots. I don't know if—"

'…the Aquarian's base struggle, the knot at the center of their being, is that of Self-Knowledge. Consciousness of Self is easy to come by, confirmation of one's being is provided constantly by the outside world, but Knowledge of Self is a trickier acquisition.

The contents of the Aquarian Self are eternally in flux, new waters flowing into the vessel, old waters flowing out. The vessel itself is all that remains consistent. The vessel is hollow. Therefore, maintenance of the vessel's integrity must be the chief concern of the Enlightened Aquarian.'

Fell in love as the truth came out: A relentless slurry in the bitingly cinnamoned malodor behind Café Destare's dumpster. Thighs taut with disaster, knees shaking blue against the cold, she poured from her bony bottom a violent sludge enough to cancel all the Christmastide in the air. Ran a dark Mississippi between her blown out sneakers, soles so thin she may as well have been barefoot. Between clod trumpeting sputs, mucous heavings wracked her chest. Snot glistened through the gaps in her shame-latticed fingers, and she said: "Don't fucking look at me."

And cut the light off before she started in on undressing herself. Early morning lightened the sky in the window, but the shadows in the room held steady, so all there was to be made out was the shrinking of her form. Puffy coat to hoodie to sweater to t-shirt, all closer, all smaller, until the oily waffle of months-worn long-johns came away like trout skin rent from flesh akin to stone. Drunk-leaning against his own doorway, unbelieving at how little he'd had to do to make this happen, like he'd somehow been chosen by the universe that night because—

She came away from his chest, after spidering her hands frantically about her twisting face, laughing. Great tearful shrieks in his empty kitchen. Collapsing to the tile floor and rolling around like she so suddenly really owned the place. Finally coming to a rest, shirt hem up just enough for him to see that beneath the slate of her belly she's still laughing.

Looked up at him standing there and: "Wait? You're serious? You're serious you thought you were an—"

'...**Earth Sign. Even among the cousins in their clade, the Capricorn finds themselves unable to assimilate. Fastidious Virgo rejects the Capricorn outright as abomination, preferring to sever the contradictory halves of the whole. Taurus simply cannot be bothered. The Capricorn is alone all the more among their family...**'

She tasted of earth, every moment of her. Tongue shot into his mouth like a lump of wet clay. Her callused hands, with their rows of tendons like piles left behind a plough, fingertips stained rusty with blood and nicotine, dug fierce into his shoulders. Lissa burying him beneath her. Kisses and falling rocks. Slate dark teeth gnashing in the night. Cloth coming away in shreds. The quivering of his skin in the moonlight. She'd bit his lip at some point. His mouth filled with blood. It dripped from her lips as she rose from the kiss she'd foundered to find him inside of her. Blood in shimmers from her chin, down her neck, and breaking out in vascular creeks over the quake-wrought hardness of her body. Granite or marble or something older—a stone of stones, the conglomerates that build mountains, the myriad rates of wear and weather, cleavage and luster, crystal and grain, a multitude of unwavering stillnesses and tremor toward cinders. Felt like she was going to break something, a wrist or whole limb or the very center of him, as her pelvis ground and ground. Stretches where neither of them were breathing. Aches building in their muscles. All softness petrifying.

"Don't fucking look at me!"

Followed her out of Caffe Destare when she left in a fury. Hadn't recognized her. Never yet seen her in light any more brilliant than dusk. Not even a place he'd usually be, too many young and hip indefinables, tattooed and pierced all to hell, haircuts like they'd lost a fight with a push mower. A rare fit of morning anxiety had sent him from his house out into the low grey of winter, dawn crushed by the heel-stomp of a year's end. Found himself scrolling through the ping and blue of Reddit, an overmilked cappuccino cooling to curdle before him, a half-eaten slice of too-sweet lemon pound cake when:

"Please!" Out of the caroling din. Animal begging cut through the forced, sepia joys, all the flavors forgotten by better seasons suddenly having their saccharine say. "Please, just let me, I don't, I don't have any, please can I just—"

Tall, shotgun-blast-faced kid behind the cash machine: "Ma'am, I'm sorry, but we've already told you multiple times, on multiple occasions, it's company policy that—"

"I don't, I don't give a rat fuck about your company policy!!" Exploded into those shrill, rasping registers reserved for cries for help. His eyes focused on her then, grating sound clearing his mind of mud better than the pudding-thick espresso concoction he'd been trying to drink. "I don't give a goddamn about your, I'm a human being and I've got to, I've got to take a fucking shit! I'm a human fucking being and—"

"I don't know. Never thought about it very seriously. Remember someone saying that I was an Aquarius and I've just kind of rolled with it. Never gave it much thought."

The laughter had by then abated and she looked up at him with all the seriousness of a blind boulder toward the sun. Sat up, crossed her legs beneath her. Face tightened as she took a deep breath. Closed her eyes.

"Never taken any of that woo-woo, mystical shit very seriously…"

'...Along with constant consideration toward maintaining the vessel, the Aquarian must also keep abreast of how full and foul the contents of the vessel have become. The potential for their gathered Conglomerate of Others to brew and ferment lamentably into something heinous is mounting ever and always. The vessel must be emptied at regular intervals, lest it fester or overflow.

Overflowing is sadly another state that many young and naïve Aquarians find themselves trapped in. This may manifest itself as exuberance, rage, panic attacks, fits of babbling bliss, or any number of uncontrollable emotional outbursts. It is not uncommon for the Aquarian youth to find his or herself singled-out and ostracized/idolized for these recurring episodes. Regardless of how these Overflow Manifestations are reacted to by their peers, the reaction will undoubtedly leave the Aquarian feeling cold and misunderstood for the simple fact that they are likely to find no source for agency or ownership toward or of the emotions at the root of the outburst, since none of the feelings poured forth have their origin in the Aquarian themselves. The vessel is still fundamentally hollow...'

"*Woo-woo, mystical shit!?* " And she stood again. "What the fuck are you fucking, what are you talking about *mystical shit?* There's nothing fucking mystical about the stars, are you insane! They're right there all the fucking time and every minute some little shit is born and you're going to tell me that that's not something that—"

"Wait, what the hell are you—?" And he backed against the wall as this newest form of explosion mounted before him. Panic and sorrow he'd seen before. Bouts of unbounded hilarity and joy were rare, but he'd still seen them. This seemingly unreasoned rage was, however, wholly singular.

"Mystical my ass, Trav. This is, this is important stuff! It's always been fucking important it's like spitting on graves to say it's, I mean are you kidding me!! This shit predates like the Bible or whatever like the first thing any of us ever thought to do, like when the sun set that first time it must have been so goddamn terrifying and then it gets replaced by a softer like the, like a different one but cooler and not as hot or whatever, the moon you know? I mean have some fucking respect! The sun sets that first day and it's absolutely fucking terrifying and the little monkey-people don't even, like there, there, there's

118

no way they could talk or anything like that so they couldn't even fucking tell each other how scared they had to have been, which had to have they had to have been so, so, so scared all of them because they were suddenly, like it had been daylight! It had been daylight and little mommy monkey-lady could look over and see daddy monkey-man and all the other little, all their little monkey-children like they were all there together and then the sun goes down and everything gets darker and, like they couldn't have known, you know? They just watch each other get darker along with the sky and everything else around them and then basically, like not really obviously, but like basically everything disappears, starts to disappear and then it does and then there's, but then there's the moon like the sun but darker and nicer and like, I don't know, slower or something and all around it, all around it where the sun was all alone all around the moon, like a whole family like the one that she thought was disappearing, all there in the sky in all these shapes that look like things down in the daylight there's all the stars and, and, and don't you fucking see how important it is that the stars are there and that they've always, they'll always, they always'll mean *something* even if—"

She stopped mid-thrust and started to shake,

caving-in around him, tightening from flesh to vice. The taste of blood hung heavy as a foundry in his mouth, hot and metallic. Boiling in sweat the both of them as her shake gave over to the sound of something small and agonized climbing up her throat. Deep, raw, meaty release as her skin pebbled beneath his palms. Vertebrae rising up like a new Appalachia, before the weathering, before the eons, before it all grinds it back down to so much sand and mud.

And he dropped to his knees beside her there, the leg of his jeans falling into the flow. He dropped and took her into his arms. Took her into his arms and kissed her dirty cheek. Kissed her dirty cheek and said: "I love you and—" Made promises to her that he can no longer remember.

Promised *himself*, though, that he would love her, that he would marry her, and that he would soften her. After they were married, she did indeed soften. Softened enough so that whenever they managed to leave themselves enough to come together, she'd rise from the mess, bruised as an overripe stone-fruit. Her hardness not worn to felt and velvet, but swallowed by a layer sweet-weeping flesh…

'In the sorrowful throes of its rank rejection,

Capricorn often feels forced to decide which half of their substantive contradiction to indulge. At worst, they sympathize with the inclination of the Virgo and begin to wish themselves torn asunder, severed, bifurcated—liberated from all traces of their inborn uniqueness. Be warned, Youth of Horns, there is no return for the Capricorn that follows sorrow and rejection to these conclusions: the splitting of your twin soul, just as in the case of your mirror-spirit Gemini, can only lead to spiritual exsanguination...'

Travis wakes at a sound. Loud enough to cut muffled through the office door. Snorted start nearly knocks him from his seat. The manilla envelope is the only casualty. Falls from his lap in a clattering coda to the shatter or shutter, crash or catastrophe, of whatever is on its way to collapse outside in the restaurant.

On the concrete floor, among the dead bugs and spent butts, edge torn by some unkindness on the way down, precious terminal papers peaking out white and innocent. A big dark sob-spot in the middle of it. Hadn't dared open the envelope. Cried himself to sleep the minute he sat back in his chair. Sobs turned to holler, great snotty gags of uncontrollable sudden grief. Doesn't remember falling asleep in the chair. Remembers holding the paper wet against his face as if it were her and not her absence that was sealed away by tongue and twine. Remembers the grief giving way to rage. Remembers rage quickly taking to his chest, burrowing behind his weak, palpation-prone heart. Remembers his chest getting hot like to explode. Remembers a sudden exhaustion and waking at a sound.

The security monitor reveals now to his tear-gritted eyes the sound's potential source. Every split of the screen hums a black-and-white hive of chaos. The front dining room teems with sloshed life. The glitter of unbussed tables mingles dangerously with the sway of drunk college student and townie patrons, impatiently rising from their seats. Not a server in sight.

A little warmth kicks at Travis' waking temples.

The bar is just as swamped. Customers lined up five deep in some spots. Cliff's behind the stick tonight for some reason Travis's slept through the revelation of. Easy to see that he doesn't have the temperament to man the bar. Kitchen skills don't just transfer like that. Glasses stacked in teetering towers. Serving beers that are two-thirds head. Blindly grabbing bottles off the shelf instead of rail.

Can feel the margins shrinking. A tingle sets about Travis' fingers.

Heart of the disaster: Love at the kitchen window. Brynn posted up there, black-jeaned ass cocked out into the walkway just begging someone to stare and drop something. She leans against the ledge, face hidden from the camera, ponytail bobbing around enough to indicate that insofar as she's concerned the whole rest of the world can disappear so long as she holds the ear of her scuzzy kitchen-boy. Will, face blurred by smoke from the abandoned grill and broiler, is paying her all the attention she can ask for, engaging her with the same gusto indicated by her ponytail and thrown hip. Love. Love. Love. Business crumbling around them, responsibilities forsaken all for this moment of heinous love.

Brynn leans further into the window, feet lifting off the ground.

Looks to swat at the smoke-softened form of Will as it ducks down.

Shadow rearrives and out of the kitchen, just nearly missing Brynn's head as she gets her feet planted, zooms a plate to shatter against the framed vintage beer advertisement on the opposite wall.

Travis rises at the second sound of shattering. Blasts out the door into the entropic din of a shift gone all wrong. Turns toward the kitchen window to find Will now leaning out, teeth gnashed, and Brynn, fists at her sides, cords roiling in her neck.

'...should the vessel break, the Aquarian will find themselves drowned in a surge of uncontained Other. Shattering their vessel, either willfully or by general negligence, is an irreversible mistake made too often by naïve Aquarians. Negligence is understandable to a certain degree, the young Aquarian is not in a position to easily find council and can be led readily down incorrect paths by the even most well-meaning of other signs. The willful breaking, however, is a grave misdeed against oneself. The Aquarian must know that it is their status as vessel that allows them to handle their position as a point of convergence, the manifestation of the essence of their being that point, but in no way is it the essence itself. Even without the vessel, the Aquarian finds themselves poured upon. It is only with the vessel intact that the Aquarian can have any hope of survival...'

7

Postulant

Music's loud. Thoughts stay small. Broken to little pieces by headachy dumb-thudding bass. It's best this way. Outside our ears all is cotton. Everything in all our brains rolls around like marbles and shake us hard enough we could be the maracas or whatever that sound is that's coming from the Bluetooth. Frazzle. Worst bathroom ever. No ventilation hardly. Ado's is much better much nicer everyone loves everyone much more at Ado's all much more the sound from the Bluetooth chopping the track up. All this steam getting into the wires. Frazzle. Waterproof as advertised. Frazzle. Cut the water. Step out into the Christ it's cold and crank this next track this one that Ado mixed and posted up for a pay-what-you-can free download all proceeds going toward their eventual double mastectomy. *Get it! Gotta have it!* in a robot voice now before the beat drops earlier than they'd normally allow. No edging no build just more and more their inclination toward Frazzle and Frazzle giving everyone what they want immediately and they said gunning for transcendence that they're gunning for transcendence so everyone hold on tight because the rocket is going to Frazzle. Damn. What is wrong with this goddamn speaker all of a Frazzle. Grab and wrap the towel and dry off the hands before Frazzle the screen all can't thumb it off won't recognize the touch now. Frazzle. Smells like spoons taste hot pennies and burnt hair. Spark and jump and lights come off. Bulb shot with the jumping blue. Hard dark and dripping from the faucets and a pipe hissing in someone else's apartment walls it's gone so quiet now. It's gone so quiet now can hear everyone else can hear the surrounding units the whole complex. Everyone else lives here too. But they only hear Ado from this apartment when the shower is running or dishes are being done or meals are trying to get made or it's late at night and the comedown won't come down and the dancing won't stop even though we're all alone and should be quiet like it is now. Can hear all of them living here though and that's no way to hear Ado. Through the walls when they're not the only thing happening is no way to hear Ado. Has to be dark and quiet and then Ado starts and then everyone can be themselves all together and the bright blue light on the counter. A tender buzz buried beneath a startle-sharp ding. Notification of a text message lighting up and it's good to know the phone has survived as advertised. Not as seen on T.V. Haven't watched a television in long enough to have never seen the guarantee so there should be no surprise the Bluetooth was a dupe. But the phone has survived as advertised. Grab it from the counter and wipe it to streaks and rainbows on the towel. Read the message. Ado's decree to the growing group chat: **BANGER TONIGHT BY THE LAKE, BE THERE TO BE REPAIRED!!!** And now a flurry of responses all begging for the exact address. All our hearts pumping in excitement because it's been nearly a month it feels like maybe even longer but that can't be right but that's what it feels like since the whole family got together to have a real goddamn get down so flip the light switch to bring it up again so we can get ready. Switch does nothing and the phone fires off hungry madness. The fuse box is somewhere too far away from right now so the phone's flashlight will have to do so hands are still so wet and now they're trembling! Be there to be repaired! Be there to be repaired! Let the music play through the phone's tinny dogshit speakers then. Set it to vibrate. Let the flashlight illuminate this whole hazy space blue like a rave stopped in time before it all began to end everything! And see ourselves shadowed in the fog gathered on the mirror beading now to jewels too delicate to do anything but cut clarity in the glass as they fall. More and more of us revealed. Our shoulders blue rocks and shadow over our sunken sternum. Bones too bent to hang muscle worth knowing of. A body worth it all now. Cut it out. Ado says they love all of us even us even though we're all so says it at the top of every show. Big low falling bomber drone. Ringlet arpeggios. A glimmering climb skyward and we follow the only words they'll say directly into the mic the only missive not buried within the intricate kabbalah of untz and scratch and build and drop and drum and drum and drum and drum that they love us all each and every one. Through the visor. Into the crowd. Each and every one of our eyes before the first track kicks our teeth in guts us and boils our brain enough to forget that when we wipe away the wet from the mirror we're left to gaze at nothing more than what we most hate. Us. All of ourselves here in the mirror as the hand comes away. The whole total shadow of self. Unignorable and present and heavy and fluidly unchanging. Can't do a damn thing about it always said that there's nothing we can do a damn thing about what we are except try and understand what it was that might have got us here in the first place got us all hateful and lit by the blue-white of a phone's flashlight. Every fossil flaw cut out by shadows. Mirror wet hand glistening with the hazy lie that hides comes to our face and finds a pustule on which to perch. A place to squeeze and drain and pour out that sticky yellow crimson-swirled pestilence that's plagued our face for as long as anyone's ever been able to see us long enough to look away. And there's that pinching pain at the pop and purge of pus releasing pressure and flowing curd to blood. Only makes it worse at a slapped away hand. Only makes it worse to pick like this but leaving it all alone does nothing to stop it. It's congenital that the flesh under our skin is always set to boil always cratering from cradling so much filth. We'll always be like this so there's no worse it can be so we'll pinch again and make it all red and scabby and like we've been shot in the face so that everyone can have something really worth looking away from and we can stay safe and bloodied in the corners of everyone else's eyes. Unloved. Unnoticed. Able to see everything from a place cloistered and away. To see is to be. To see it to be. To be seen is to fade. So keep it that no one sees us or loves us or touches us if they don't have to and we'll disappear. To join is to disappear like the hat and rumble now as kick and synth rise and speed to swallow all that the song's thus far been. And then our body will be lost to other bodies limbs all a mired briar with the rest and the bliss will come because it always does with hours melting into nothings all a moment wracking our bones to sweat and powder and we can forget. We can all come to forget that our bodies don't fit together and we're all ugly to everybody that none of us are made in the image of anything other than everyone else and they're all just as hammered and chiseled and worn away from themselves as we are and all there is is to find some way to become something that everyone can love so we wash our face now. We wash our face and scrub and scrub and scrub until every mound and crater breaks out from pus to blood and wash it off enough so that it cakes around our eyes when it dries and runs up pennies into our nose when we start to sweat. Oh god oh god to sweat. And take the gag to silence ourselves before we become. Take the gag a size too big to stretch our jaw to render every utterance the truth a biting pain and drool to carve rivers in the glitter we'll slather on our chest. All to become. All to become none. Not one. Not one with everyone but none like everything. To relinquish this humanness that's hung haunted over us for all our life lived too long. Relinquish the visage and condition that makes us one of the hated by everyone including all ourselves. Relinquish it by becoming that mindless drooling toothy thing loved by all but the worse. Loved even in its death. Loved perhaps then most of all in its absence because everyone loves other people's dogs and other people love their dogs more than even themselves and other people. Love them enough to wash them dead. Poor boy. Poor poor boy we'd heard him say there in the mud. I love you poor boy my poor poor boy. And he ran a rag of suds over the ribby short-haired flank. No rain but the hose was running running the lawn to muck and silt and even he seemed to be sinking under the weight of such a corpse. Fresh enough to still be limp tongue hanging out of its butcher's arsenal mouth. Tiny eyes closed. Washing the body bereft of soul. But dogs have no soul and that's what there is to love about them. There's no pit to the peach. It's all just fruit. People have too much rind and too many seeds to spread.

Washing the body hollow as it was when it was alive but now still and honest forever. That's the way to be loved by everyone. Everyone worth loving loves dogs. So we wash the humanness from our face to bleed like everything alive. Gag up our mouth in moaning silence. Cover ourselves in glitter to shine like far off stars where there is nothing close enough to worry over. And put on the snarling mask of a wolf enraged. One to body to something to love and lose. And we all lose. Lose and gain nothing but sound and loss enough to know that a return only spoils the next track. The blessed same again. Return so the bass can reassemble the rise and collapse. The cycle. The safe same. Hat and snare and kick. Synth and pitch. Yaw and thrust. Momentum toward dissimilation. Transcendence to a plane unimagined for its impossibility. Unexplainable for its nonexistence. Blissful for its absence. **BANGER TONIGHT BY THE LAKE, BE THERE TO BE REPAIRED!!!**

8

Anchorite

Hopes for a twitch. Sat crossed with the bulk over his knees. Flanks still and limbs falling back limp. So, so heavy.

Buster'd sniffed. Smacked his foam-strung jowls. Rory rolled a nibble of cheese around a pressed-and-stamped lozenge. Tail a baton batting bruises into Rory's shins. Buster's stiff-legged good-boy jig, excitement running rebar through haunch, shoulder, and spine. Rory's hands shook and set to sweat. The pill powdering to paste at the edges. Cheese all to grime at the heat. Buster let loose a big ol' *Boof!* The goodest boy Rory'd ever seen. Dropped his rump to the ground—sit and wait, tail slapping up dust, just like he'd been taught.

"First things first," Rory said kneeling the doorway of their previous apartment. The newly re-christened Buster's collar chain wound tight across his knuckles, steadying the brute to unclasp the leash the shelter'd spotted him. Said: "First things first, welcome home, buddy." Slapped the dog on his backside at the release. Sent blazing over the apartment's stripling and warp-split wood floors.

Not an ounce of regal 'Leo' in him, none of the noble lion indicated by the staff-bestowed name on the cage. This rescued bundle of muscle was all a blustering Buster: big, sweet, smiling through every pant with crazed-over, cooped-up, and love-starved geniality. A Buster from the minute Rory'd seen him through cyclone fence, prying his heft from a cold concrete corner, approaching the come-hither finger head hung low, a prostrate plea hopeless in his eyes. Sudden reeking piddle once the finger found its scritch on his dewlappy chin.

"Wanna take him out the yard?" The shelter worker trailing Rory's trudge down the corridor of cages shouted over the din of desperate barks and yowls.

The Yard: a vast slab, split through by cracks and

crabgrass, mounded on moldering occasions with plopped piles. Fearful, excited puddles shot the cloud-clotted daylight back to the sky. A few others taking canines for a spin, little yappy things mostly. A family with a readily agreeable mutt. On the leash Leo was slow at Rory's side, a stride behind, head still hung.

"Can take him off and let him run around if you like," said the attendant worker.

Rory dropped to a knee and unlatched the leash. At the release Leo remained still, eyes flitting down, then back up. Teary and glistening, haunted. The tarsome turgidity of a chronically melancholic mind. Rory rubbed up behind the flop of an ear too big and loose for its blocky bear-trap face. At his touch, the gaze dropped away.

"What kind is he?"

"Best we can figure's probably pit and basset, maybe beagle. Something like. Definitely lots of pit though, can't deny that."

Rory's hand ran the short stock of Leo's neck, over his cinderblock chest. Leo readjusted his footing, a step away to build the distance. Bored by it all, like he'd been through this too many times for hope to have a hovel left in his dumpster-dog heart. "How old?"

"Three at the most. Probably two. Gonna be big. Still a puppy…"

"So calm for so young."

So, first things first: Freshly freed Buster set to sniffing a gusty whiff of everything. Sneezed every couple steps, clearing his snout new to the best of the rest. Feet couldn't decide which direction to go. Got caught in a circle before turning a lippy grin at Rory in the doorway. Rory held out his hands and Buster bolted back to him. Slowed at the fingertips, dropped his head, tail tucked, sniffed, and darted off again.

Tried not to take it to heart. Knew that the happy guy was just floored to finally be out of his cell and into a forever home. Wanted to explore and get to know where he'd live out the rest of his days joyous, cared for, and fawned over. Had to take it all in, so Rory stood to close the door and took a seat on the edge of the coffee table. Leaned forward and just watched the wagging slab, unaware that this distance would become the way of things. The gap between them, Buster's skittishness around hands, would never manage to close over the next year and some-such months. Always away, curled up on his dog bed or propped on a seat unoccupied. In his next apartment, this studio where everything that's fallen to pieces gives over to crumbling, Buster took to sleeping on the floor next to Rory's bare mattress, but never once indulged in the mattress itself. However unclosing the physical space, though, Buster's eyes never left Rory for long—flitting back from away and, if their eyes meet, that tail start banging against whatever was nearest, all Buster's folds tightening into his grin. Would follow Rory to the kitchen, wait outside the bathroom, follow a step behind on walks. Always calm, quiet, crestfallen—except for those first few moments in his new home and whenever the promise of food was apparent.

"Fuck," Rory said and rose from his spot on the table's edge. "Food." Hadn't thought to buy any, was just excited to get Buster home to fill a hole unhollowed. A whim satisfied. "I'll, uhm," there was a grocery store a quarter mile walk away, "I'll be right back, bud. Just—" talking to him as new roommate, not separate species "—just don't bother your Mama, alright?" Rory pointed to a closed door opposite him, "Don't bother your new Mama just yet, ok? I wanna introduce y'all."

It'd been a week—though he'd done everything he could to forget when the procedure had taken place, the day and time still knelled in his head, tolling the the accretion of days since, the thrust forever into a future of guilt hanging heavy from everything. Not the life he'd imagined. Not the promise. A week and she'd yet to leave the bed save for sudden trips to the bathroom, rocketing through the apartment. A brutal antibiotics regimen, hollowing her further every day. Couldn't bear to rise otherwise.

Rory reached out for a pet before leaving. Buster rolled out of it.

&

Ran out of dogfood again earlier this week. More and more, longer stretches of time where all Rory can afford to feed Buster is the scraps of scraps. Money goes like whey through cheesecloth. Servers tipping out the kitchen just enough to keep management off their backs. Paychecks every two weeks, but state and federal take their cut. There's just not enough. Bills have stacked and she can't be bothered to talk about the unbroken lease. Can't pay for the sty he's stuck in now, much less a rat's nest unoccupied. Won't talk to him at all anymore. Fair enough. That's fine.

Buster didn't rise to follow him to the fridge this morning. Seemed to know it would be empty. Didn't stop Rory from looking over his shoulder, stepping aside to show the lit up void, and mouthing words of apology.

Though Buster didn't lift from his pallet beside the bed, his tail did offer a single wag. His ribby chest inflating a worn-out bellows. Understanding there in the droop of his eyes. Knowledge.

But what could he have known? Could he have known that Rory couldn't just steal food again? That every time he slinked around Village Mart, that five aisle convenience store a hundred sidewalkless yards away, every minute mounted suspicion. That only cans could be stolen? And only so many? That he needed more than that even for himself? Hefting out a some-such pound bag of dogfood would be impossible and Rory's not got the legs for running.

"I'm sorry." He says again.

Head falls to Buster's shoulder. The short fur there has caught the drafty studio's late winter chill. Scant flesh beneath the skin still holds a little of life's warmth. Fading under the trickle of tear, brown spots of Buster's coat lose their luster and run toward mud, all the white grays. No heartbeat in the cavern. Not a kibble-scented breath left.

Hopes for a twitch as his crossed legs fall asleep, toes atingle. Hopes that it didn't take. Seems like something that couldn't possibly have happened—just a thought, a horrific and brief whim like the unshakeable urge to jump when perched on a cliff-ledge. *What-ifs* will be, though, if brought full forth as *is*. Fantasy is an inactive realm, the moment it's made it's rendered indelible and now Rory can feel the break. Buster's head lolls in his lap, internally severed free from all the rest of himself. There in the flesh like a root vegetable snapped in a grocery bag.

His whiskers are white. Nose dribbling its last as the pebbled tissue chaps. His whiskers are white. Never noticed. A hand. Stiff prickle on callused palm. The hand shied away from. Lifts the lip, a muttering foam, and there's the teeth. Yellowed and caked at the base along the gum. A fierce canine chipped. When did that happen? Always been like that? Never noticed it in the smile. A thumb on Buster's brow opens a peacefully shut eye. Brown against the bloodshot white. Always thought them black, beady, buried...

Bought the biggest bag they'd had. Walked it back thrown over his shoulder. Sweat stung his eyes as he climbed the stairs. Dropped the bag on the floor. Skitter of kibble through a burst paper seam over the tile. Buster nowhere to be found. The bedroom door open a glimmer crack.

Rory rapped with a knuckle before pushing through into the bedroom to find the two of them on the bed. Buster's head resting on his new Mama's belly, the rest of him curled at her side. Her hand atop his head, rubbing the worry between his brows. Tail slapped the sheet at Rory's peaking in.

She stared at the ceiling. Asked: "What's its name?"

Three days and she joined them at the table for breakfast. Scratched the wagging rump and, "G'morning, Buster."

Rory looked up from his overcurdled scramble as she sat in the creaky folding chair opposite him, "Good morning, babe."

She smiled. Small. Her cheeks were hollow, gray in the face.

"Hungry?" Rory returned the smile and spiked the fork into a burnt-yellow clot. Brought the fork up and over the edge of the table to where Buster sat begging. Sniffed, licked, and the wad came unforked. Dropped to the floor to be gobbled up.

"Don't do that." Reaching across the table to pluck a bit from the mass for herself.

"Do what?"

"Feed it at the table like that. It's bad training or whatever…"

"Who says that?" Rory turned the plate so that the pieces of the meal that hadn't been pecked through already were closest to her.

Another bite between her fingers and a huff, "Oh,

I don't know. Don't remember. Saw it on T.V. or something... Should just feed him dogfood, though—"

"We're out."

"Didn't you just—"

"I know, eats like a bulldozer though. Just a big ol' big boy!" Leaned over the table to try and rub the praise into Buster's face, but quick as ever Buster juked.

"Can't get all up in his face like that either, Ror. They don't like it."

"Since the fuck when," voice blooming toward boom in his throat, "since when do you know anything about dogs?"

She broke from his gaze. Lips tightening toward white, biting the insides of her cheeks. No tears. Not this time. Not ever again, actually. "I don't. Just heard stuff. Never had one, but just, don't know. Don't know anything about dogs... I just..."

Buster's head cocked curious as silence fell over the meal. His tiny, beady eyes, black in the light rising toward noon through the window, flitted from Rory and the plate to where she sat opposed, rubbing her thumbs into her palms. Anxious tick.

Buster's nails clicked over the kitchenette tile and his head came to rest in her sweaty hands.

"I'm sorry," Rory said. "I didn't mean to, you know I don't, I've never, it's, it's been a long time at least. I'm sorry. I…"

She disappeared beneath the table's edge. Brought her face close to Buster's and squinted into small, talcum-dry giggles as he slathered his tongue over her cheeks.

When she rose, Rory reached across the table, pushed the now cold plate of eggs out of the way, and wrapped his hand around her wrist. "How are you feeling?"

Eyes back to Buster. "Better. Feeling better."

"Good," and an attempt to lace his fingers through hers. A moment and, "I'm sorry."

"For what?" Thumb of her free hand propped up Buster's ear. Rub in the powdery pink warmth.

"All this, I guess. All the—"

"It's not your fault."

"I feel like it is. I had a part to play at the very least."

"Eh, not worth getting bent up out of shape about. Happens. Always happening. Caught it soon enough."

"Just barely."

Buster's tail was wagging. He sat again. Rory couldn't see, but he knew he might be smiling.

"Just barely is soon enough. No one's fault."

143

"It's hard," Rory let her hand go. It left the table and found a place in the fur. "Hard to know that we ended something—"

"Kept it from starting. That's all."

"We—"

"*I*, Rory." Again down to Buster's face to offer her cheeks for licking.

The little he'd eaten flipped in his belly. Heart summersaulted. Heat glassed his eyes.

"You should get more dogfood today... There should be a little left in the account if we're still out of cash..."

&

The hope for a twitch is shot down dark. Chest hasn't heaved, its last a moment forgotten in tears, and the quiet that hung in the air after the snap, shudder, and cease has begun to fall like precipitate out of a solution. The room comes back around him.

Twiddling Buster's cold ear between index and thumb, Rory scans the ruin he's rendered for himself. Clothes shellacked with kitchen grease all piled where he's had drunk occasion to leave them. A path cut through the refuse from the bare mattress to the bathroom. A crusty towel hangs from the wrack therein. Dishes piled high in the kitchenette sink, a jumping froth of flies hovering. The smell. A gaggy reek—the effulgence that spills from fester turned over to bursting.

So, he'll bury Buster out back where the grass climbs to bramble before falling all hillsome to a forested gully. He'll bury Buster where no one can see because he can't just add him to the trash. It was mercy, had to be. It has to have been mercy because he couldn't have just taken him back. Can't start over and can't have, they wouldn't have let him, they wouldn't have let him put him down. There was nothing wrong. And besides, just like all of this, just like all this it's always all of this about money. They would have wanted money to kill him and he couldn't pay for, woudn't have been able to bury him then either maybe so this was the best way. Bury him then out where the ground is soft and he can be put deep, deep, deep down like he'd never been asked to be anything other than mud. Never hungry or scared or good. Just mud.

"I'm sorry," and again Rory's sob-swollen face descends to the limp in the neck. "I'm so, so sorry, Buster."

A sniff to clear his nose, smells like he was never loved. But he was, Buster was loved. Smells like all the rest of what's piled around Rory. Neglect. Cowardice. Entropy. But, Buster was loved and Rory knows that. Buster was loved and is loved still so, so, so before he buries him, he'll wash him. Wash him of all the failure of life and prepare him to be mud. Take care of him best he can after the intracted fact of it all.

Death was the only way. She knew that. She'd come to terms with it all much earlier in life than he'd ever had the chance to. Sweat breaking out, an honest panic at the word—"Positive." And the bedroom door shut behind her. Test dripping in hand, she leaned against the desk. The whole room between them.

He'd wanted to rise from the edge of the bed, take her by the hips and into his arms. Hold her close, safe where he'd always told her she'd be safe. Close was too close to what had put them here, the whole room between them. Touch never the same.

"What, uhm, what do we do now?"

She told him what she knew:

Clinic. Testing. Imaging. Questions. Waiting. Days waiting. Back to the clinic, maybe a different one, who knows. Dark. Procedure. And he'd have to be there as escort. There to walk her in and wait. There to walk her out. And then: Ruin. Didn't have next month's rent stashed away. More hours, he'd have to ask for more hours and she'd get a second job, something in the world like him to offset comma-pushing online. They'd both have to work more to pay for starting fresh and hollow. Keep it or shuck it away, things'd never be the same and that was ok because:

"Shit happens." And she'd known it always could.

She opened the door and held it for him the day of the procedure. Signed herself in, filled out the paperwork in stern silence. Returned it and crossed her arms. Watched the fuzzy whatever that played on the television hanging high in the waiting room. Rory breathed beside her, all he could think to do. Wanted to grab her hand but she rose at the sound of her name. Nodded at the murmuring nurse. Disappeared.

An hour, tops, and she reappeared in the waiting room. Nurse's hand on her back, looking for her escort. Rory rose and she was handed off to him, to his care, to whatever safety his arms could provide. She said she was woozy, tired. Leaned into his shoulder as they left...

Woozy. A worry in his eyes. Could tell that his feet beneath him were getting heavier, because that's what the pill was supposed to do. Make everything heavier so the world around could lighten and lift away. Smacking his lips for the bitter and the cheese, eyes rose to Rory. And trust twitching the worry along his brows. Rory sat on the bed and held his hands out. Couldn't remember what the pill was but remembered forgetting what it did. Took one at a house show months ago, blacked out and woke up the next day as happy as a puddle could be. Bought three from Will, who enumerated its uses and articulated its pharmacological moniker. Took one then. Took another the next week to wash work away. Saved this one for the later that would become now.

And it worked: Buster trudged the space between them and rested his too-heavy head in Rory's hands. Even began to climb into his lap. Rory scooched himself off the bed and onto the floor. Buster curled there in his lap. Breathing slowly. Eyelids falling and blasting back open. Pupils frantically searching before resting on Rory's face. And the lids fell again.

Rolled the relaxing mass onto its belly. Not a moment of resistance there, complete surrender, absolute faith within the haze.

And Rory scratched at Buster's upturned chin. Traced the length of his neck where under the skin jaw gave way to throat blooming out to chest and shoulder. Opened his hand. Found a hold. Squeezed hard as he could through the rolling loose flesh.

Tendon and trachea and the slightest tightening against his fingers by muscle drunk on pharmaceutical miracles. Harder but his fingers kept slipping. Couldn't find fast enough to cut anything off, so he released and applied pressure to the throat with his elbow. Rolled off once, twice, before it found center and something inside gave a moist crack. Buster stiffened and shook, legs kicking as pain overtook the effects of the drug. Foam on his lips and from his snout, some rasp choked approximation of a horrified bark. Kicking and twitching and twisting out of Rory's hold, Rory pulled him closer and shifted. Shifted the trauma-tightened neck so that it spread over the cross of his legs like a board over cinder blocks. Pressed the heel of his hand between skull and shoulder, pressed the whole of himself into the writhing drool until he heard a snap.

And stillness.

So, now he'll wash him and he'll bury him because this is not how life is supposed to be. Then he'll drink and take whatever is given to him until the lights go out. He'll live as careening dead, make sure to wake up on the other side as soon as he can, where the last promise is said to lie.

9

Kyrie Eleison

A breeze to cut the falling heat curdles lake water a black film on her belly. Second skin breaking over the quivering rise, every breath a fissure through sanded scuzz. Hands, tingling at the tips, dig into the pebbly shore to ground her. She's becoming solid again. Back to where she'd let go. Been out of in the earth for too long, can't yet uncurl her toes.

Sun's in her eyes but she dare not close them. Let the gathering tears dilate the light to a truthful hue. Don't blink it away. All dry on the outside in the wind, so protect whatever wet's been given. A lick over her lips and the lake is there. Tastes vegetal, of algae and all those drowned trees; mineral, like sand or concrete.

He'd poured it into her after she'd wrestled him from the water.

&

Oatmeal had just started to bubble between stirs when Travis said, "Good morning, lovely." Hands on her waist, tender belly against the small of her back, pushing her into the—

"Hey! Hey! Watch it!" As he brought morning breath and scruff to her neck, her stomach—now a tummy tumescence, spare tires and love-handles—touched the edge, hot from the gas burners. "Trav! Goddammit!" A singe through her t-shirt.

Release and, "What? What? What did I—"

And she spun around, hackles raised at this ever-shrinking cage, "The fucking stove is fucking hot! Can't you see I'm fucking trying to make some, Jesus Trav just for once like—" turned back to the pot, away from his falling face, that pathetic wane over cheeks as his grin collapsed.

"The hell, Lissa?" Could hear in his voice that he'd taken a step back, retreated. "What's up your ass this morning?"

With one hand she stirred the thickening slop; the other she pressed against her stomach, over the rising swath of burn. Though fabric separated her hand from her belly, it was clear how much softer her touch had become. Her palms had once been pebblesome. Her stomach an arid plane of sandstone, warped and wefted impenetrable muscle. She'd once been like all that would be left at the end.

"What's the matter?" Travis asked, voice choked and cottony.

"Nothing." And Lissa spooned half the cinnamon-raisin mass into a bowl. Found a spoon in the drawer and stood it up in the thick. Turned then, holding it out to him.

He stood against the wall, twiddling his thumbs, looking at his feet and ruined sneakers.

"Here," she said. Bottom of the bowl already too hot on her hand. She pressed her fingertips in harder, baking back callus—clay in a kiln.

Travis looked up, eyes to the offering. Back down and, "I, uhm, I can't actually… Got to get in early today, there's an order of, there's a shipment coming in and they've been mucking up the invoices lately and—"

Just walked away. Chickenshit. Heard the door shut gently behind him. Coward. She took the bowl to the nook and sat. A spoonful on her tongue like a dirt clod, and she heard the sedan pull out of the driveway. Silent then save the sound inside her head: tooth and tongue mushing the mass into her cheek, throat closing against it. Appetite totally lost. It's all just too easy. Can't tell anything through the kitchen window but that the daylight is new. Could be cold. Could be the hottest day on record. No trees to account for the breeze. It's all just lawns and vinyl siding. All kept to keep the world at bay. Walls.

She hung her face over the bowl and let the glutenous clot fall back into the hole it had been carved from. She rose.

"Well… it sounds to me like you're doing quite well." Her mother'd said when Lissa hadn't realized she'd called her.

"I am. Yeah." Was all Lissa could get past her teeth. Would have been a waste of time then to count the years since they'd last spoken.

The night after their courthouse ceremony Travis had given her a slip of paper torn from a lined notebook. On it was a phone number. He implored her to call it, said it was important for their life together. At that time, in a state of captive rescue, what other choice was there but to comply? The previous winter had been the coldest yet.

When the phone picked up, the voice on the other line said: "Hello?"

Lissa asked, "Who is this?"

A name was said. Then: "And who might you be?"

She'd not expected the tears. Recognized the voice immediately: Menthol gravel and the thick smack of too much lipstick, a gas-station-pastry sweetness beaten to the cream down at the bottom of her register, bubblegum in every sigh. Lissa didn't speak for her lips' quaking. Eyes hot. Face hotter with embarrassment, rage, and grief.

Her mother spoke, taking the snuffles through the line as evidence enough that this was the call she'd been promised by that man who said he was going to marry her daughter. She said: "I miss you." Paused. Little click on her end. Speaker frazzling exhale as she took the first drag of a blessed cigarette. Then she said: "Tell me about yourself."

If she could have muscled through the collapsing star of her face, Lissa would have told her mother that it was springtime, starting to warm up but still a chill in the air, and that night had come on early and heavy. That she was sixteen going on oblivion. That as usual she'd asked him to pull onto the shoulder just beyond the super's double-wide, where the dirt gave over to grass and perpetually dying rosebush. She'd never explained to him why she didn't want him driving on into the flickering orange lamplight.

Never told him it was because she didn't want him seeing where she and Mama lived at the back of the park, abutting the swampy woods. If he'd ever begged the question Lissa would have told him it was because Mama and her boyfriend didn't want her dating, wanted her to focus on getting good grades and getting into college or something like that. Luckily, he never asked. Lissa suspects he'd have spotted the lie. He would have asked her why her grades were so bad then. She wouldn't have had an answer.

Like always, he did as he was told, and the rose bushes scraped against the driver's side of the truck. Lissa unbuckled and shifted to open the door. His hand grabbed her backpack strap.

"Wait."

Faced him again at the behest of his pull. "Yeah, what's up?" Heart skipped there at his shadowy face.

"Not gonna kiss me before you—?"

She shot across the gearshift and planted a quick one on his lips to shut him up.

No sooner had her lips left than his hand found her neck to press them back in. Caught cocked on her hip at a strange angle, held there as his tongue worked its way into her mouth. Over-chewed gum and wintergreen snuff. Thought for a second to bite, send him back to himself bleeding, but the hand was harder then, digits working into the base of her ponytail.

A muffled moan from somewhere deep in his throat and he pulled his face away from hers. His breathing was heavy, fogging up the windows. Spit glossed her lips. Mustache and fuzz chapped her chin.

"Y-you, you know I love you, right?"

"I, I, uhm…"

"I love you, Lissa." And that look that men's faces melt into when they don't get their way and don't know what else to do but force it. "I love you. You know that? And you just, you're just always so—"

"I love you, too." Again she went in for the kiss. Easier that way. Seen plenty of times with Mama and hers what happens when language gets brought into it. Seen plenty of times how tenderness can turn its teeth.

Moved in slowly, alleviating the aching hold on the back of her head. Softly on his lips. A hand on his chest, over his heart. Fast beneath coat and ribs.

"Please, please," he muttered against her unwavering kiss. His hand lifted the bunching bottom of his coat and set about his buckle. "Please, please."

She pressed in harder then, all to silence him.

156

But again, "Please, please, please." And a grip wrapped round her wrist and brought it down.

Found him there, hard up and aching on her palm. "Please."

Out of the truck, it clotted between her fingers and dried to crackle across her knuckles. He'd made her bring him to surrender. Small moaning hiccups between the spurts, face of a crying baby breaking out between glassy eyes and twisting mouth. Groaned that he loved her over and over until, "No! Stop! Too much! Too much!" through the pouring sop and slapping her away. That look of so much spilled shame.

She walked down the dirt and gravel roads that cut through the trailer park, holding her hand by her side as far away as a limb could be made and still kept.

When she came to her and Mama's single-wide, Mama's boyfriend was slumped asleep on a lawn chair. Shallow fire pit smoldering, bottles strewn about. Knew her walking by would wake him. Knew even if it didn't, he'd wake her: stumbling in, slamming the screen door, and feeling around in the dark for Mama. She'd wake to him *pleasing* and begging and by then it had all been enough so she turned back and rest became what it has been.

Didn't know where she intended to go once she

was past the plot's entrance. The state-road went off in its twin directions. Exit left was town, exit right was whatever happened to be next. She kept to the shoulder. Bent down at one point to foist up a handful of pebble and dirt. Rubbed it between her hands to scour away the scum left by his sudden softening. A few cars passed, none honked. She eventually came to a service-station. Borrowed a phone from a freckled clerk who looked sick of lending out the station's phone to vagrants. Lissa couldn't have looked particularly roughshod at that moment, other than the dirt on her hands. Called home and left a message saying she was going to be gone from now on.

If she could have relaxed her grimace, taken her teeth from their gnash, to shape the words she didn't have, Lissa would have told her mother that it wasn't long before she'd wanted to come back. It had only taken her a month or so to cut herself deeper than she'd ever thought possible:

Scrounging in a dumpster behind a restaurant three counties west of where she'd left, her hand had passed over a sharp and clear shard of broken something. Didn't initially feel it. Took the gunk gathering on her palm as wet waste from the black plastic wrapped welter. Got her fingers on something bready and seemingly whole. Pulled out an unseparated loaf of burger buns greening at the edges. Noticed in the bug-husk clouded light the dark sheen of a substance she initially took as ketchup. Its blot had climbed her forearm, smeared and growing. A sledgehammer's wallop swelled through her body. Over the scent of garbage came a waft of hot penny and sweaty iron. Shifted to catch her palm in the light. Sludge erupting slow from the mount of Venus, flooding the plane of Mars. Her mouth went dry. Vision blurred. It all stopped to dark. Woke in the morning to the sound of tires on gravel. Blasted up from her place on the ground without so much as a glance over her shoulder. Just ran, hand glued to her sweater with dried blood.

The next several weeks she'd spend pushing further west, against this dizzying defeat. If she could have stopped the tears and snot from pouring for a moment, she would have told her mother how she had to get further away because turning back would have been too easy. She would have told her mother how she purged the wound of its cottage-cheese curdled pus in service-station restrooms, onto train tracks, behind bushes wasting a bottle of water over the gash, and in the bathroom of a travel bus she'd stolen someone's ticket for, until the yellow mush bloomed to fresh, dark blood. A bandage improvised from a pilfered athletic wrap served well enough until it started to crust and its elastic gave out. No matter how often she purged it, how quickly it managed to scab back over, the heat and surge would soon return. She lost use of the hand, ache rolling to numbness. Digits swelled and purpled. Whole right side of her body hot with fever. Just couldn't pour all of it out. There was always more festering. It made her mind boil…

She woke in a hospital bed. A scythe-curve of thick, black stitches ran from the base of her pinky, over the thumb's mound, and three inches down her wrist. She woke again to a nurse and a paper cup of pills. Antibiotics, the little churned woman shook and implored Lissa to eat something. She woke once more again wracked with evacuation, insides all dead and leaving.

"You've got a visitor," the nurse said from the door days later.

Lissa would have told her mother that sweat broke cold all over her body. She grabbed the sheet to try and throw it off, but her arms were weak, her body a mile behind her mind. Her impulse was to run again, fear dropping its lead grenade into her stomach to blast flack and fire. Lissa would have told her mother that she was terrified that she'd have found her and taken her back to life under the heel. If she could, she would have told her mother that the kindest person she'd ever met appeared in the doorway:

"How're we feeling, sugar?"

Lissa's knees came to her chest, kicked the bedpan a slosh. Confronted with this woman who wasn't who she'd feared she'd be, Lissa's brow hardened, scowl sharpened, back straightened.

"Figured you wouldn't remember me none. Eyes didn't barely open when we found you." She came to the bed. Under the fluorescents it was plain to see how she'd caked her edgy, crinkled face in rouge and dark foundation to round herself kindlier. Blue bruises of eye shadow, clumped lashes. Her smile a wind-blown conflagration. "That's alright, sweetie. Just glad to see you're still with us. Ain' seen so much blood since my monthlies stopped up. You was in a bad way, you know that?" A long-fingered, veiny hand came out to grab Lissa's risen knee.

Lissa let the hand stay. Knew this type, harmless and hollow boned. Nothing to worry over save the saccharine stick of her words.

"Didn't manage to catch your name, hon. Couldn't get you to speak."

"Lissa." She'd said without meaning to.

"Nice to meet you." And then she said her name.

A hefty mess of syllables her kin must have thought beautiful. She followed it with a less clobbersome sobriquet. "You know anyone we could call to tell we got you here? Family or anything?"

Lissa's mouth was shut, unwilling to spill any more secrets. Would have been the end of it all if she'd given anything away. Looked her age, and that was no age to be out and about bleeding alone.

"Alright, reckon you've got nothing to say. That's just fine…" She sat then at bed's edge. "Doctors and all said you're free to go, they can't keep you here n'more and, but you've got to have someone take you out since you seem a minor. Said they couldn't find any identification on you or nothing, searching for missing persons reports now probably and—"

Again, the sweat broke. The urge to run.

"—See in your eyes, now they're open and bless are they beautiful sweetheart, you ought not be laid up in a place like this with eyes like that. Bet every boy counties over from wherever you think you're running from's got themselves a mighty crush on you, bet you go back and be real happy with one of them… See it in your eyes, though, that you've made up your mind and you ain' going back for nothing and lucky for you I ain' the woman to tell someone what to do, specially if their face looks like they've got good reason to do what they're already doing. But they's saying you can't stay here no more and got to take these pills with you and take them a little longer, make sure your hand don't blow up again. Said your brain was all swole up too there for a bit, like to call yourself lucky for living…" Shook an orange pill bottle. Dropped it into her gator-skin purse and smiled. "I told 'em I knew you, friend or family they didn't seem to care none, just want you out, only ever care that I'd take you out of here to where you needed to go… So, where is it you need to go?"

Silence. 'Anywhere' wouldn't have been answer enough. 'Nowhere' would have been a lie.

"Alright, sugar, you stay shut up, that's just as fine as anything else for now. I know a place might be nice."

If she could have settled to remember, she may have told her mother that this woman's car smelled exactly like her own. Pine air-freshener, smoke, fast-food cheese. Told her that the land surrounding the roads they drove on, though flatter, was in no way fundamentally dissimilar to where Lissa'd run away from. That in her haze she either hadn't made it very far from home, or that the hard reality was that their home was no different than anywhere else where people ate poorly and too often…

They pulled into the parking lot of a roadside diner, truck-stop shanty sort of place. Greasy windows, a sign that no doubt flickered in the night, potholes in the asphalt to comfort cars cattywampus.

Once inside, door not yet shut behind them, this woman shouted a name toward the counter, followed it with, "Two breakfasts, hon, the works and everything! All y'all got and I know y'all got all of it! Little lady here is starved to bits!"

They sat in a booth, across from each other. Lissa's gaze on her lap, her shredded palm.

Quiet other than the bustle in the kitchen, kicked up by the order barked. A pinch-faced teenager came by with coffees.

"Let me see your hands, honey."

Lissa did as she was told, placed them on the table palms up.

"Hmmm… It'll heal up fine enough I bet." She curled her hands over top of Lissa's, covering the fingers and squeezing, "You remember at all yet?"

"I don't know what you're—"

"You's here about five days ago. Middle of the night. Come in out the rain and sat in this booth. Wouldn't talk to nobody or anything. Little miss

164

with the coffees here tried to take your order and ask you if you was alright and you didn't say nothing. Looked like hell turned over. Seen roughed up girls before, honey, been one myself, but you was in a way I ain' seen in some time…"

She went on. Told her how she'd found her in the bathroom after. Had her son kick the door in, so that lock'll need replacing, and found her on the floor, dirty floor that time the night too, after all the long-haul boys have come in to empty and refill themselves. So much blood they'd all thought she'd hit her head, but found pretty quick it was that messed up hand there. Like to have died there on the floor if it weren't for someone trying to take a squirt just in time. Know that? Like to have died and that's not what she wanted, the woman said she could tell even through the sadness and fear in her eyes that death wasn't what Lissa was chasing after. Could tell that death's what she thought she was running from, and far be it from her to stand in the way of a young woman what wants to live. But she knows, known it long enough to stay alive herself, that certain things got to get taken care of if a life worth living through is to be managed and, well, running around bleeding to all hell isn't one of those things what ought to be prioritized, so just, what's meant to be said here is—

Then the plates came. All piled high and steaming. Two stacks of pancakes. Eggs and bacon and grits and a basket of biscuits and Lissa couldn't even remember what all else even if she'd had breath enough to recount it to her mother.

The plates were brought across the arms of a young man, acne scars quarrying the beautiful range of his cheeks. He set them down and turned away, but the woman grabbed him by the apron string.

"Not so fast, not so fast!" Grinning.

He rounded back, eyes down and shy.

"Here Lissa, this here's my boy, my son, he's the one what deserves the credit and I think ought to be thanked first and foremost."

Lissa's stomach was growling as a 4×4 coming out of a mud sink. Mouth watering so much she slurred her speech when she said it: "Thanksh…" Trickles of embarrassment welling in her eyes.

"You're welcome, Miss. Wasn't nothing but a thing…" His voice was deep, newly rich from aging out of his youth, like overused fry oil.

The woman spoke then: "Son, this is Lissa. She's gonna be staying with us for a while. Want you to be nice as you should be to her. Like a guest and a lady. Nothing but respect. You hear me?"

It was her place, the diner. Despite the disrepair it

was a nice place to be. Lissa would like to have been able to tell her mother about all the people she got to meet working behind the register and balancing plates of eggs, hash, and meatloaf. That little nothing hole-in-the-dirt was situated near the interstate, so she got to know someone from everywhere. Heard every story enough times to figure out at a preciously young age that they're all basically the same. Came to the realization, as she listened to truckers smoke through their coffee, families bicker their breakfasts cold, couples old and young cut the silence with smacks and slurps, lonely travelers indulge always in just a little extra sauce on the sundae, that the ultimate tragedy of it all was that everyone lives in the same place, everyone's in the world and no one's got an honest escape plan.

The owner's home was just down the road, far enough so that the interstate's roar was swallowed to a hum. A squat ranch-style house, cyclone fence to demarcate her death-splotched plot of grass from all that surrounded it. An apricot tree dwindled out front. A plastic swing-set sun-bleached out back. Lissa was given a room she was told was for guests, but the décor—pallid pastel wallpaper and filigree, clean white everything else—suggested something more like a nursery. It was on the other side of the house from the diner owner and her son's rooms, separated by a small kitchen, dining, and living room. Lissa was told she would have free range so long as she was respectable. Lissa would like to have been able to describe it all to her mother, just to let her know maybe that she'd at least once, for a short while, witnessed what a home was supposed to look like.

The son, who manned not only the kitchen at the diner but damn near everything else his mother wouldn't manage, was finishing a GED program. Studied hard it seemed. He was little seen by Lissa outside of the diner, even though they lived less than four walls away from each other. When he was seen, it was most often through the kitchen window: a working ghost, compliant and sweating, never a cross word from him, always a nod and the feline focus of his hazel eyes. His form was all angles, sharpened by labor's physical rewards. He was not a large man, but he was sinewy and hard. Scruff, scrap, and scrape.

When Lissa couldn't sleep, she would stare at her closed door and try to listen. Her mother probably wouldn't understand, but if Lissa could have told her she would have said that sometimes she felt like she could maybe hear his pencil scratching well into the night, hear the wet part of his lips as he read silently to himself, hear his joints pop as he stood to stretch and reset into his study. In reality it was probably all imagined in the quiet. But, everyone lives in the world they've imagined for themselves...

By the end of the summer he'd left home. Got his GED and moved to an apartment complex closer to town. Lissa stayed with his mother, saving the little she was paid to maybe one day follow him or set out again for herself. She still saw him through the kitchen window. Until she didn't.

One day, someone else was in the kitchen. Some grumbling other who took cigarette breaks every thirty minutes despite how many tickets were hung on the rail.

"Hey!" Lissa said through the window the next time his hazels came. "Where, uhm... Where you been?"

"Oh, I been around. Busy." He said. A grin gathered, then fell. His eyes darted away and back and, "Why? You miss me?"

Lissa's cheeks flushed, palms set sweating. "Yeah, no, uhm... The new guy is just, uhm... can you push table four's waffles? They got a kid raising hell and—"

"Sure thing."

End of the shift and he come up behind her as she reconciled the money with the register and herself.

"What're you up to for the evening."

They'd lived in the same quarters for nearly eight months before then, both a birthday passing by without fanfare, but never had she been anywhere near this close to him. A heat came off of him. A high onion sweat, some earthy musk at the bottom of the fragrance that had Lissa's mind shaking to scramble.

"I don't, nothing I guess. Just was gonna go back to your Mama's and maybe sleep or something."

"Still all you're doing, then? Working and sleeping? Ol' Mama still got you locked away and all?"

Lissa shut the register and turned around. Never noticed the inches he had on her, used to seeing him slumped over the grill or leaning down to the window, bending to the will and necessity of something else.

"Not locked away, no." Crossed her arms and tried to straighten up, but only got more of his chest in her view. Looked down and away. Gazing upward felt like it'd make her dizzy. "I can go whenever I—"

"You wanna come and, come over and have a drink maybe?"

"Come over where?"

"My place, Lissa. You ain' never seen it. Maybe you see it and you can tell Mama not to worry so much no more. Come see it and tell her I'm doing just fine."

"Uhm…"

"You'd be doing me a favor."

The apartment: a chronically dusty sort of place. The garbage cans were full, kitchen a disaster, carpet piles stiff. Ceiling low.

"Brew?"

"What's that?"

"Beer? Want a beer?" And he disappeared into a kitchen yellowed by smoke.

"Uhm, sure."

"Have a seat anywhere, make yourself comfortable."

There was only the couch.

If she hadn't known the house he grew up in, she never would have guessed it. It was like she'd fallen backward into the trailer. All in disarray, all chaos, all surrendered to the will of entropy—just making the trip to rock bottom easier hammocking one's home above the crag.

The couch cushions were hard.

He came back with two cans. Cracked one and handed it to her. Sat down. Cracked his.

"TV?" And motioned to the black box at the other end of the room.

"Sure, sure, uhm…"

Remote. Click. Color. Sound.

They sat. Drank a bit. Then she spoke: "Are you gonna be working tomorrow?"

"Yeah, but at the new place. Got another job, more money and—"

"What, where?"

"Construction stuff. It's grunt work but it's alright. Getting on well with the guys in charge so maybe soon I can—"

"You aren't going to be working at the diner anymore or—?"

"Told Mama I'd do Sundays. I can do Sundays. Gives me Saturday off, six days a week, one easy one before the real work starts and, yeah. Sundays. I do Sundays."

"Oh, I guess that's—"

"No more work talk, alright? Let's just relax and…" He sat forward and reached for a frog-shaped cookie-jar on the peeling coffee table. Opened it, decapitating the frog, and produced a plastic sandwich bag with five or six white pills inside. "Let's just relax. Do you mind?"

"I don't, no. Don't suppose I—"

"Great."

Pocket knife. Stoneware coaster. Chopped the pill across the median. Placed the other half back in the plastic bag. Blade flat and crushed it all to clumps.

Rolled the glint until it was all powder. Organized the dust into three lines. Leaned over, nostril plugged, and sniffed. One. Two.

"You want any?" Held the coaster out to her.

She'd smoked enough cat-piss and belly-button-lint grass back home to know that nobody shares anything that's particularly powerful, especially chronic users. So, Lissa nodded and plugged her nostril in kind.

Didn't quite snort hard enough. Smeared more of the powder into the stone with her nose's leading edge than she managed to get stuck up into the soft vascularities she was aiming for. All for the best perhaps, on account of the little she'd managed to get up in her kicked in immediately.

Was like her skin flew from her. Big gold ball of warm goopy something swelling in the pit of her belly, some soulful pregnancy nine months of which would have amounted to a moment. But the chill at its edge where the skin left, fluttering off in tatters, rags, or crushed autumn brush. The warmth met where she'd felt her flesh exposed and spilled out. Warbling mirage of radiated heat against all cold everything. The world far away as her skin, hot blood and sunshine. Bliss, something like what bliss had to be like.

Hadn't realized her eyes were closed until something fell into her lap and brought her back. Room all still brown and unclean, but dirty like loam or mud or freshly tilled field. The television blurted its rainbows and the absurdity of having something to say. Lissa's eyes fell and found him there, resting his head in her lap. His eyes were open, glued to the television. He inhaled through his nose irregularly, as though something in him had forgotten he needed to breathe, as though something in him had ceased caring for continuation. He was smiling.

This was better than the high.

She'd mostly come down by the time an hour passed, but his head stayed where it was. His breathing slowed more but had evened out. The small smile faded into a soft-cheeked face of contentment. His eyes closed when she began running her fingers through his hair.

This was better than the high.

He melted into her. Knowing that he was feeling something similar to what she had just come down from feeling herself, Lissa felt confident that insofar as he was concerned her touch was completely a part of his being, down to the glowing core of it all. He was warm water cupped in her hands, free for her to splash wherever she pleased, pour wherever she'd want filled. He was hers to drink. She was the only solid thing in the room.

Things between them went on like this for who can say how long, Lissa only knows it was cold outside when it started and cold outside when she ran off again. She'd come over most nights of the week and watch television with him as he liquified himself. Eventually they would come to consummate their feelings physically, but sex was nothing in comparison to his absolute surrender. He was too much another person, full of desire and need, when they coupled, his body making demands of hers. She never managed to come once in their clumsy thrusts. Made enough of a show of it, though, to quicken his finish. Then, hollowed by release, he would crush a pill and snort the whole thing. She'd hold him until they were both asleep.

In the mornings when they both had to rush off to work, he'd grumble about taking Lissa to 'that bitch's restaurant.' In the evenings, picking her up from her shift, he'd rush her into the car all 'come on, come on, I can't fucking stand this place.' He never saw his mother much, all updates as to how she was doing came from Lissa. The fact that she'd not had a bad word to say of the woman irked him endlessly.

"If only you knew." He groaned up from her lap

that last night. Rolled over so that he was looking right at her. His eyes were red from forgetting to blink, lips chapped from mouth-breathing.

"If only I knew what, my sweet?" Could see that the drug was fading, setting him back as solidly in the world as she was.

"If only you knew what it was like to grow up in that house. My Papa left us, you know that?"

"No, I did not." They'd never talked much about their lives. His Mama never mentioned her own either, seemed to prefer concerning herself with the goings-on of others.

"Yeah, yeah. I had a daddy. I did, I did. Remember him being a very big man, big and silent. Not that he'd have had much room to talk none with that old bat flapping around the cave. Bitch."

Hated him when he was like this. Coming back into the world all edgy and sharp. Brow crinkling inward to ball up the fists in his mind. Hated him for having this side to him. Had gotten worse and worse. The moments he was out from under the influence he quickly hardened into a hot ball of lead, sizzling and taking everything, the whole world, as an affront.

"Did you have a rough day today or something? What's the matter?" She ran her fingers through his forelock, greasy curls then wet with the sweat that was beading up on his brow. "Did you—?"

"Every day of my life has been a rough day, Liss. That's what you don't seem to fucking understand. Never ever had a single easy day in my—"

"Shh... Shh..." Leaned down to kiss him quiet. "Here, here now." And she shifted out from under him. Reached for the first time into the cookie jar herself. Seen him do it enough times, figured she could manage it. From the bag she took two pills. Crushed them up on the coaster gone white from use. Piled it all up in a clumpy line. Turned and held it out to him. "Here, baby."

He was sat up on the couch, head in his hands. His face rose, red as a busted plum, vein cleaving the plane of his forehead. There were tears in his eyes. The heels of his hands were wet.

If she could have staid her throat past anything but quaking, filled her lungs without aching, and set her tongue to say anything, she would have told her mother that she didn't mean for it happen like this, really she didn't, and that it was all, please, please, please trust her, it was all an accident. If she could ever manage at some point in her life to tell anybody, any single promise-shut soul, she would say that she was sorry and that she'd never seen a man sweeter...

She left him twitching on the couch and foaming at the mouth. The thought of too much hadn't ever crossed her mind, the pills were so small.

The money in her pocket, piddling tips from the day's shift, got her a bus ticket across a few state-lines. She'd never heard of the town she bought the trip to and hoped that that meant nobody would think to look for her there. The asphalt was iced over when the bus pulled into the depot. Lissa stepped gingerly through this new place as to not hurt herself again.

The depot was at the edge of the town. Could see indicators of its sprawl from the terminal windows—telephone lines, salt rock gritted roadways, trees grown shrubby, and the blocky breach of squat buildings' rooftops. The sky was purple in the night. Clouds low and threatening snow catching the little city's lights. It was cold in the terminal. She'd only had the clothes on her back and not enough cash. She sat on a bench and stared out the window. Time passed, how long she wouldn't be able to say but Mama would have understood that it doesn't take long to notice that people are looking at you. Gotta get going at some point, loiter around and someone in uniform will make the decision on your behalf.

Lissa stepped out and started walking. Once again she'd found herself on the shoulder of a state road, only this time trudging toward where she thought town might be, not in the direction she knew it wasn't. As she walked, the leafless trees disintegrated, steadily replaced by homes, then businesses. The businesses clumped together into car-chocked plazas. Soon homes were replaced by apartment buildings and everything replaced its siding with brick and before she Lissa looked to realize the sort of place she'd put herself she was knocked to the cement by a clucking flock of blondes.

"Oh my god, I'm so sorry!!"

Hands on Lissa's shoulders as she lifted herself from the ground. When she rose, Lissa came face to face with the most perfectly perfect face. Not an ounce of life showed its line as the young woman twisted her lips to continue her apology.

"Are you ok? Are you hurt?"

Porcelain smooth, rose pink on her cheeks. Lipstick, eyeliner, and whatever other mess Lissa'd never learned to apply. Even the streetlamps were kind to this woman's features, they didn't cast clownish shadows or set her in ghoulish relief against herself.

"Yeah, yeah, I'm fine. Watch where the fuck you're going," Lissa said, wiping the grit and pebble from her hands.

"Hey, I said I'm sorry, I didn't, I just—" Lips tightening their way to a scowl.

"Yeah, whatever just fucking watch it." And Lissa turned away to continue on.

Head up then she noticed the streets of this downtown area were swarmed with people of similar stripe to her collider. Puffy black jackets and leggings. Blonde. Blonde. Blonde. Young men in coats and spotless, name-brand work boots crinkling up the cuffs of their jeans. Hoodies sporting a logo composed of three letters. Everyone joyous and young and screaming. She'd wound up in a college town, bussed in on a weekend night.

The frigid bacchanal dizzied around. She wrung her cold hands together as anxiety mounted about her shoulders and bit ears. Thought her hands were wet from sweat until she looked down at them and realized she'd spoken false when she told the pretty lady she was fine. Lissa'd caught her fall with her bum hand, scrapping it up something bad on all the quartzy salt-rock. Sticky blood. Hadn't noticed it. Nerve damage from the previous year's wound. Would have told her mother that it's been long enough now she doesn't even notice she doesn't notice it.

Lissa ducked into the nearest bar. Luckily, no

bouncer. Unluckily, the lady's room line wrapped all the way around the pool table in the back. Lissa made to dart in, cut the queue, but was held in contempt.

"Excuse me," arm out to block her as the door broke its flush with the frame, "there's a line, what do you think you're doing?"

"I, uhm, I—" Lissa couldn't find the words. Fear frothed her mind. The close call with regards to her injury the previous year was not lost on her. If something like that were to happen again, if she were to hurt herself and poison her blood, break herself beyond her ability to repair, she wouldn't be able to rely on dumb luck and kindness.

Lissa held out her hand.

In the dinge it looked like it'd been run to bone by a cheese grater. The injury was nothing severe, but the girl at the head of line shrieked nonetheless: "Oh my god! What did you, what did you do to yourself? You poor thing!"

A thing. A poor, poor thing. Unable to preserve itself, some poisonous thing with ruin in its wake and chaos at its hip. Radioactive. If she could have managed it, she would have told her mother that the girl, who couldn't have been much older if she was at all, pushed into the bathroom, taking Lissa by the wrist. Pushed through all the gossipy gather, hip-checked a sink clear and immediately set to washing Lissa's hands. Warm water and soap and a question of does it hurt. Lissa shook her head as the mud-caked blood was cleared away, shook her head that no it didn't hurt like it should. Can't for the life of her remember what this young woman's face looked like, one of many in a sea of similarity.

Got honestly drunk for the first time that night. Lissa's new friend stayed by her side and kept the drinks flowing by flirting their way down the bar. She asked Lissa questions, and Lissa lied through her ever-widening smile. Said she was student too. Undeclared major. Then the stories flowed: re-stitchings of the babble she'd overheard at the diner, strung together to make out a rich and broad life to shawl her shoulders. Learned that night how listening can get you anywhere, how people pour themselves out for anybody, and if you can catch some of it you can pour them out instead of yourself whenever asked for honesty...

It landed her a roof over her head and breakfast the next morning. A shower. The works. A hangover the only drawback.

"Alright, Liss. I'll see you around! I've got to hit the library for some studying so..."

"Yeah, yeah. Ok, cool."

She walked out into a crisp winter day. Sun out and low, long shadows and everything cast in silvered gold. Everything was quiet. Felt like a Sunday. She moseyed along the sidewalks and smiled at how wonderful this place was. Nothing seemed to be falling apart, nor did it threaten the possibility of it. Everything was maintained.

It was cold, though. Lissa dug in her pocket, nothing but change. Maybe enough for a coffee. There was a shop down the street from where she was. Caffe Destare. She went in. She didn't have enough for a cup, not even a small. She jingled the coins in her fist as she walked out with her head hung dejected.

A voice like gravel and burlap: "Spare some change?"

She looked up and found before her a begging clump of hair and dirt.

"I can't," she said, "this is all I got right now."

The man smiled beneath his beard. He shook one half of the grimy fishing vest he wore, producing the dull metallic rattle of coins in a pocket. Said, "Same," and went on his way.

She didn't know then, but his name was Jeremiah.

The winter went its full way through before she had another moment face-to-face with him. Until then, he hovered in her peripherals. Shaking change on street corners, digging in garbage cans, sat shivering on benches chowing on half eaten refuse, or dragging his feet with a forty in one hand and a moan about his mouth. Lissa avoided eye-contact as much as she could, afraid perhaps that he would come to recognize her as a comrade. It took her a week to scrounge together a change of clothes. A few items were shoplifted, but most of the others were from boys' homes. She'd quickly mastered the grift from her first night in town and it kept her off the streets until the spring when the light winked brighter, the days lengthened, and sweat slicked skin again, caught in fabric, stank its way a heaven higher. Young men were easy, though.

Prospects for work dried up whenever a potential gig asked for identification and tax information. Lissa was sure she maybe could have gotten all that together if she really wanted to, but the fear was still there that she was being looked for. All the more then considering that she'd absconded with the possibility of a body behind her. Back to Mama's house was one thing, prison another. Managed decently enough on the alms of horned-up and drunk college boys. A roof over her head most nights, food ordered in or breakfasts out to remove her from the house. The usual favors were requested and obliged in satisfactory fashion. Secret was to make sure they drank just as much as they thought she did. A fumbling drunk was easy, softer, to manage than a man whose night had gone according to plan. Most often they'd fall asleep, unable to become erect or to finish. The hope was to get them sick enough that performance of any kind was impossible. She didn't like their touch, made her feel small and tender, breakable. When they did fuck it was always fast and clumsy, labored and unsatisfying. They slept next to her like tuckered out puppies in cupped palms. Discovered that with regular trips to the bathroom, finger and throat to send the last drinks up, she could stave off entry into the darker regions of intoxication. Then they'd be putty in her hands. This all, however, what with the clothes she managed to steal from them, gave her wardrobe a tom-boyish affectation. Occasionally a woman would come on to her, reading preference into her basketball shorts over long-johns and work boots. She'd tried it once or twice, but women were difficult. They were wary and aware, less willing to lose their footing for someone new. Women were like Lissa—Hard.

Anonymity dies in routine. By the time warmth threatened its return she was getting turned away at the door from places where word had gotten around. She was recognized in the street a few times, caught in the lie. Once she stopped someone she'd stayed with a week before and begged him for change. Lissa ceased being recognized as someone people hadn't met, and was immediately clocked for what she was. Wide berths were taken around her, eye-contact lost, mutterings and pity pattered. Her stomach got used to being hungry and she accepted the haze of malnourishment as a standard feature of her consciousness. She slept where she could find and not be found.

He woke her one night:

The cardboard had barely kept the rain off, so there wasn't much sleep to fly from her. Woke wide and toothy.

"What the fuck do you think—?"

"Inadvisable sleeping in the rain like this." And he threw the soaked square to the side.

Lissa couldn't make out any features other than his shadow in the rain and streetlamp.

He bent to pick up her bag of clothes and clink. Threw it over his shoulder to join his own soaked provisions.

At this she rose, fists at her side. In this moment it dawned on her that with her numb hand she could very possibly rock someone off their feet and feel nothing in return. "Give me my shit! What are you—"

"Come with me," the man said. From this vantage, glittering eye to glittering eye, she could make out his bearded face, catch glimpse of the harmlessness about his cheeks. "You'll catch something here, sleeping all in the wet like you are. Plus, this area'll flood if this keeps up. Happens fast. Come with me." He turned away, heading out of the alley and onto the street.

"Where are we going?" She followed. The choice was made as it dawned on her how cold she was.

"Shopping plaza up the road. Sleep in the breezeways tonight. Take you to somewhere better tomorrow."

"Take me somewhere where?"

"Better!" He was hoofing it. Ducking down in the rain. He'd known long enough the lessons she was just beginning to learn: Life is a delicate thing, and there's a little monster inside of all of us that wants to keep it going. This little monster is passionate about this and only this and perfectly willing to shatter life's fragility all into a million pieces if it means the monster can get it into its wretched little hands. The monster can't be trusted with the thing it wants, so you've got to be careful to keep it at arms-length and close to your chest, maintain life yourself. Satisfy the monster that way and—

He went on and on as Lissa lay on the concrete, falling asleep under a mat of wet hair. His words sounded sure, like he'd either said them before or had never stopped saying them in the first place. She couldn't tell whether or not he'd stopped talking after slumber found her again. It was the sound of his voice that once again woke her.

"Alright, we've got to get stepping. C'mon." Jeremiah—he'd told her his name once they managed to get out from the rain and under the plaza's breezeway—rose with an urgency that Lissa's mounted hunger disallowed her. "Sun's up, rain's stopping more or less maybe, but they're all coming. Anyway, let's step. They gotta open and shop and do all the things they do keeping the monster fat and happy. Cops too, cops everywhere wherever there's shopping being done and, yeah, let's step, let's step, step, step. Somewhere safer. Get you rested and then tomorrow and everything—"

Just kept talking as they walked. Behind the beard the babble wouldn't stop. Mania or excitement, Lissa couldn't parse. Wasn't listening much, but the thrumb of his voice calmed something inside of her.

The sureness of it made this all like a life being lived and not a death being run toward.

They walked and the town fell away. Greenery rose as curb gave to grass against cruel roadway. Lissa's stomach groaned. Her lips hurt, chapped ragged. Mouth was dry. She couldn't speak against Jeremiah's outpouring of pontification. They stepped away from the road at some point, passed through a mess of bush and briar. Then, before them it all opened. The forest.

An inhale and Lissa closed her eyes, squeezed them shut until the hurt in her belly forced them back open. Then, as the pain faded, there was the forest.

Pain and the forest. Walking. Tied together, knit tight and balanced.

All the lie because none of this rose for the sake of anything other than itself. Vines don't hold the trees up and the trees don't give the vines something to climb. No. The sun is way up high, right? The sun is way, way up high.

Since the sun is way, way up high and the tree needs to have the sun, then the tree goes way, way up high. The vine, though, needs the sun as well so it climbs the tree but given the opportunity, the tools, the power, it would just as soon chop it down.

So it is with everything, though. It's all agony, screaming verdant anguish. And it was beautiful.

"You listening, girlie?"

"What's that?" Her voice came ragged, shaken, dry.

"You listening to me or am I talking for nothing?"

"No, I'm, where are we?"

"Safe. We're somewhere safe. We're where everyone ought to be but the dead. Town is for the dead. This is where life happens. All this growing and dying and one thing becoming something else and something else all falling away to feed the thing that it used to be, can't go backwards, you see? Can't, there's no way to, everything keeps on going and going and going and holding onto what is now is impossible because if it is, it was, and if it was it can no longer be. That's the law. That's the just whole complete, one-hundred percent, no questions, law of it all and girlie, you listening to me? You hear the truth I'm speaking to you or—"

"Yes, sorry. I just," She'd stopped her stepping. Leaned against a tree wooly with ivy. Hands were tingling. Dizzy little buds blooming behind her brow. "I'm just hungry and I don't—"

"Oh heavens! She still gets hungry!" Jeremiah motioned around as if the forest were an audience. "Hear that? She still gets hungry! That's the little animal, little monster inside so scared of dying it might just kill you and, here, here, here."

He slipped his bag from his shoulders and dropped to his knees. Unzipped and set to unpacking everything.

"Bound to be something for the little monster in here."

Out came bottles and cans, pieces of clothing so stained and tattered they couldn't have managed as rags. A few plastic baggies, powders and leaves. A glass pipe. Crumpled pack of rolling papers. And—

"Ah! Here. For the little monster some—" Sugary snack-mess wrapped in cellophane.

Lissa ate without tasting.

He showed her the way of life. Discoursed ceaselessly about the world-made versus the world-created. Held his fellow man in glorious contempt, explaining everyone away as grist for a mill they didn't know they'd built. Preached over upon over about his own escape from it all, his own triumph over the will of the animal and the entropic making of the world.

The conviction he had made Lissa feel by turns sure and safe in his presence and, on the hungrier occasions, terrified. How she'd come to hitch herself to his wagon, she couldn't quite figure. He was constantly present, though. Always around, begging for alms and talking the ears off students smoking outside the coffee shops and bars. When she'd trudge through town, having succumbed to the fact that panhandling was the only way to acquire food that wasn't literal garbage, he'd appear and rope her into a lecture, share the substance he'd somehow managed to acquire, split whatever vittles he'd scrounged. She could tell by his eyes that he was falling in love with her. All men, even the scuzziest sages, get the same look on their face when overcome with pathetic infatuation. When the sun would set, he'd appear again to guide her toward whatever area of the forests the unhoused had decided would be the night's sleeping ground.

She obliged his desires one night, three-weeks after he'd plucked her from the rain. Around a fire of twigs and leaves Jeremiah had set in on a diatribe about the nature of hard and soft things, getting hung up on the soft quality of fluids, water in particular, and its ability to render over time even the most solid of stones as mirrors of its flow. This was a contradiction that increasingly flabbergasted him the more he spoke on it. While he mulled between utterances he would take a pinch of some powder from a small plastic bag, compressing it between his index finger and thumb, snort it hard, and rub the residue over his gums. Every little bit more brought counterpoint to the fore.

The day that led up to this night had been one in which Lissa had not managed to eat. Her stomach was starved past growling, instead pouting petulant in its emptiness. She was light-headed and furious. Wanting to sleep but too hungry to close her eyes. Jeremiah had offered her a pinch of whatever it was he imbibed, but she turned it down. Powders scared her. All fine and messy. Once they were in, they were impossible to get out...

The fire dwindled to embers. In the fallen darkness Jeremiah's ranting kicked into an ecstatic register. Without the burden of seeing her face, with only the simple knowledge of her captive presence, he twisted his words into a high, kaleidoscopic nonsense. It flew from his tongue evangelically. His pentecostical spew cauterized Lissa's mind and, with no room in her thoughts for reason, she lunged across the ashes and tackled him out of his charismatic rocking.

Could hear his head hit the forest floor's hard pack. From his mouth jumped a howl, some great *Selah!* to Lissa. It was the most horrible sound she'd ever heard—worse than the foamy gurgling on the couch, worse than the pathetic groans in the boy's pickup truck, worse than her mother's smoke rasped moans of discontent a wall away, worse than anything. The sound was the pus from her palm, the hatred of this failing body, the wracked purge of ill-fed bowel, the curse of living at all spoken in one gagged syllable.

She put her left hand on his neck, pressing past the beard and digging her fingers into the tendon and cord. She wanted to pull out his throat, to silence him. Just another man too full of himself to realize he's talking too much, just another man who saw her as only some soft thing built for him. Enough. Enough. She should have done it in the truck years back. She should have done it on the couch when she had the chance. Just end the bastards. Want hard? Solid? Impenetrable? Edge? Granite or marble or something older? Want a stone of stones, the conglomerates that build mountains? Myriad rates of wear and weather, cleavage and luster, crystal and grain? The multitude of unwavering stillnesses and tremor toward cinders?

Under the press of her palm he still managed to speak, now asking for more. Outright begging her for herself now that she was so close to being his.

Shut up. Shut up. Shut up.

She dropped her face down to his. Hissed into his open mouth. Teeth gnashed. Growling like the animal inside.

"Please, please, please." Again! Again! Begging all

breathless. Pathetic little failures every mind they've got. "Please."

She brought her lips to his. Jeremiah's lips closed on hers and his hands grabbed the back of her head. He sucked her tongue past his teeth like a lump of wet clay.

Face held then against his, Lissa balled her fists and laid haymakers into his ribs. Hollow sound of the drum drumming. His grasp on her head loosened and where there had been moans there was then whimpering. She decoupled their lips and lunged back in to bite. Give gave over to a coppery purge. The taste of blood flooded her tongue. Soft. Soft. Soft bleeding, pleading man.

Her hunger shifted, rolled its neck and reached for a new avenue of satiation.

Slate dark teeth gnashing in the night. Cloth coming away in shreds. The quivering of his skin in the moonlight.

Kisses and falling rocks.

Blood in shimmers from her chin, down her neck. Breaking out in creeks over the quake wrought hardness of her body. Blood on his face, a shiny smear matting his beard.

He was sobbing and she took him.

They lay on the ground, naked, side by side as the

sky above them lightened. Dawn was coming. The night sky had been clear, but a front was rolling in. The gathering clouds wept over them.

"Precipitation." Jeremiah said through a thick mouth. A breath that rattled like an engine sputtering for fuel and, "The whole world. Precipitate out from the solution of chaos. Falling to the bottom. Everything that was once one now divided into so many so much else. Can't puzzle it all together, something's lost in the clumping. It all just falls from the mixture, the pure truth unstirrable. Can't mix it back enough to drink. It just piles at the bottom. The whole world just piles on itself. The world piles…"

All of this, though, was then beyond her tongue. She's never since been able to tell her mother any of it. Everything they've shared since then has been on Lissa's part an invention. Every moment of her life as her mother knows it is false. Life is easy enough to invent. Men are easier.

Lissa cried into the phone until her insides dried and then, listening to confirm there was still breath on the other line, she said: "I am married to a very nice man named Travis. He—"

Just walked away. Chickenshit.

It was hotter than it ought to have been outside. Spring haze still hanging over the lawns, bound to fry away within the hour. Summer come early, always earlier it seems.

&

A breeze to cut the falling heat curdles lake water a black film on her belly. Second skin breaking over the quivering rise, every breath a fissure through sanded scuzz. Hands, tingling at the tips, dig into the pebbly shore to ground her. She's becoming solid again. Back to where she'd let go. Been out of in the earth for too long, can't yet uncurl her toes.

Sun's in her eyes but she dare not close them. Let the gathering tears dilate the light to a truthful hue. Don't blink it away. All dry on the outside in the wind, so protect whatever wet's been given. A lick over her lips and the lake is there. Tastes vegetal, of algae and all those drowned trees; mineral, like sand or concrete.

He'd poured it into her after she'd wrestled him from the water.

Acknowledgments and Further Thanks

It is a blessing that nothing is done in a vacuum. Everything worth doing is done with and for others. Were it not for this fact, this would all be so much mumbling. I have many people to thank.

First is family:

Phil & Tonya Jost, thank y'all for putting me here, providing, and putting up with me. To my brother Andrew, thank you for sharing your childhood with me. May we continue to grow closer into our adulthoods. Grandparents: Jeanette & Henry Jost, Georgia & Alvin Howard—Thank y'all for my parents and for the memories in which so much of my work finds its foundation. Opa, we miss you—Hope you're proud. Love each and every one of y'all.

The teachers I have had over the years, both during

incomplete times within educational institutions and outside in the world they warned me of, are too numerous to list with any degree of totality. These names and thanks will have to suffice for now: Tony Willis, for your red pen and kind words. Bruce McConnell, for your lessons on the nature of change. Matthew Pivec, for your early encouragement of discipline as fundamental. Ben Rice and Frank Smith, y'all taught me ears before I knew how to listen. Melody Eotvos, for calling my bluff. Tyler Damon, for showing me the way. Herbert Marks, doubt you remember me, but you retaught me how to read… I'll never forgive you for that. Andrei Codrescu, thanks for the brief assurance of my path, sorry I disappeared, hope to talk soon.

Now… Friends, to whom I owe the rest of everything:

Alex Hunter, Kyle & Steven Impini, Braden O'Keefe, known y'all longer than anyone else. Thanks for sticking around, for the support, for the friendship; means more than words can say. Hope we can all keep doing it, got lots more ahead of us—heard life can be pretty long if you're lucky.

Lyn Rye, never go away. Please.

Alex Aguirre, brothers for life, end of discussion.

Cesar & Dave, let's have a drink soon, and another, and another, and another, and—

Trevor, where you at? Hit me up. Let's start a fire.

Andrew Links, dear friend and collaborator, here's to the beginning of a big thing.

Thanks to Miette at Whiskey Tit for helping a dream come true.

Special thanks to Stefan O. Rak and Aria Wetzler—you know what you've done. Family runs deep. The Organization is strong.

Also, if a God is there, they deserve no small mention.

And Lou, I love you.

About the Author

K Hank Jost writes fictions. He believes that language is the only remaining commons. He was born in Texas and raised in Georgia. He moved to New York City in 2018. He lives there now. He reads. He writes. He works. He did not finish school, but he reads. He writes. He works.

About the Publisher

Whisk(e)y Tit is committed to restoring degradation and degeneracy to the literary arts. We work with authors who are unwilling to sacrifice intellectual rigor, unrelenting playfulness, and visual beauty in our literary pursuits, often leading to texts that would otherwise be abandoned in today's largely homogenized literary landscape. In a world governed by idiocy, our commitment to these principles is an act of civil service and civil disobedience alike.

Made in United States
North Haven, CT
20 March 2022

17352063R00117